MR SIXPENCE'S FAT BANK BALANCE

(NON EXISTING IN THE HIGH STREET BANKS)

FICTION

By Elina MARTIN

PREFACE

This is a book about a man who had a very funny character. Mr Sixpence, though a husband, hardly met the characteristics of husband. Though a father, he was very far from it. Even as a neighbour, he hardly knew how to be a good neighbour.

Prototype is Job, from the Old Testament in the Holy Bible.

Most of my stories are from personal experiences. During my childhood days, my father's friend had similar characteristics and that's where I got most of the ideas to write my book.

CHAPTER ONE

As Shelly was going through her mail, she was surprised to receive a bill of £51.60 from her uncle, Mr Sixpence.

She could not remember owing money or borrowing money from her mean uncle. She quickly grabbed the phone and dialled his number. The youngest wife answered and Shelly was told that her uncle was out in the back garden attending to one of his dogs which had just died. She knew what that meant. When his dogs died, he never buried them but would carefully remove the fur and cut it into pieces in preparation for their next meal.

Shelly dared not leave a message for Mr Sixpence because he never returned calls, let alone phone anybody. Mr Sixpence always used any tricks, clean or dirty to save his money. Lina, his youngest wife told her he would be free within the next hour and requested she call back at five in the evening. If she phoned later than five, she might not get anyone as Mr Sixpence's family retired to bed at six o'clock daily.

At exactly five o'clock, Shelly rang again and was answered by her greedy uncle who was readily waiting for the money she owed him according to him.

"What does this £51,60 bill you sent me, mean?" asked Shelly, as she was really worried and also confused.

"It's the money for stamp and envelope plus the food you ate at my house last week when you visited me. Do you still remember last Tuesday, when you came to see your sick auntie. I want my money back within the next two days!" Mr Sixpence exclaimed.

"You are very crazy, uncle. You mean to say I have to pay for visiting you, but how come when you visited my mother you did not contribute towards any expenses incurred?" asked Shelly and by that time she was really getting angry.

"Don't ever compare me to your mother again, okay! She is very stupid and she allows everybody to use her. I am not an idiot like her. I said I want my money back or I'll come there to collect it myself and then you will also have to pay for my travelling expenses," and he hung up the receiver.

To avoid hurting her mum's feelings, Shelly wrote a cheque for the amount stated by her own uncle who by the way was married to her own mother's sister and she posted it that very same evening.

Mr Sixpence was the meanest, most greedy person anyone had ever come across. Just imagine, charging his own niece living expenses and yet the farm where he lived belonged to Shelly's grandmother. During her long illness which led to her death, Anna, Shelly's grandmother wrote a will which left the farm to Angela who was her eldest of the two daughters she had. The younger daughter, Anita, Shelly's mom, could not go on the will because she was born blind.

Everybody always thought and believed Mr Sixpence married Angela for the farm. Shelly's grandmother's will had also stated that Angela take care of all her younger sister's expenses. Since the death of her own mum, Shelly's mom had only been given a cheque for £29,00 on the day she was buried and nothing else not even a birthday card because it seems her presence above planet earth scared him. He actually preferred her to be six feet under.

In actual fact, Mr Sixpence owed Shelly and her mom a lot of money but nobody dared argue with him.

Even after Shelley got to marrying age, she never did because she had to continue caring for her blind mother.

Angela was Mr Sixpence's oldest wife. Besides Angela, Mr Sixpence had sixteen other wives and they all lived on Angela's farm. Between the seventeen wives, they had a total of one hundred and sixty –two children. Mr Sixpence hardly remembered their names and luckily enough for him, they all had his body features in one way or the other. There was no way anyone could steal his children as they resembled him and had little or none body features from their mothers.

Mr Sixpence had this one policy and it was never to spend any of his money but spend other people's monies instead.

The irony was that as bad s he was, Mr Sixpence's dad had been the First bishop of the Christian Church. With a good background like his, people expected Mr Sixpence to have a lot of good manners. But as it seems, Mr Sixpence was referred to as the Mayor of Sodom and Gomorrah. Negativity was his motto. Besides being mean, he was also very cruel to his own self and his wives and children.

Two of Mr Sixpence's blood sisters were nuns at a local Catholic Church. Mr Sixpence was the black sheep of the family.

Several times Shelley had tried to sue him but her mom always stopped her. Anita, Shelley's mum had many rights to the farm but as Mr Sixpence stated, Anita was very stupid. The thing of it was Anita did not feel like adding more misery to her sister, Angela, who had to put up with her husband's sixteen other wives plus their numerous children.

Little did Mr Sixpence realise that Anita was only acting in the best interests of her one and only sister, Angela. The main reason he kept marrying was that he wanted daughters only and not boys. In the little town of Zabhera, where he lived, girls brought riches to the family the moment they reached the marrying age.

Marriage in Zabhera involved the boyfriend's parents giving plenty of cows to the parents of the wife to be. The more daughters one had, the richer they became.

Each time one of his wives gave birth to a baby boy, Mr Sixpence immediately looked for another wife. Eventually he ended up with ninety nine girls an only sixty three boys. Mr Sixpence really wanted all his children to have been born females.

It was said that a long time ago when Mr Sixpence's parents turned fifty-nine, he took them to an old aged home. This was done so he could sell their house and keep the proceeds for himself. The previous year he had tried, they were refused because the old aged home only took pensioners and pensionable age was seventy one. As he was so desperate to get rid of them because he did not feel like maintaining them financially, he dyed their hair white so they looked old and that is how he finally got rid of them. The trouble was he had to keep dyeing their hair and one of his wives heard him plan to end their lives.

When he visited them Christmas time, instead of him bringing them gifts, he went specifically to get the gifts they had got from Santa Claus. He also took the opportunity to steal gifts from the pensioners sharing the dormitory with his parents. These were the gifts he gave his own wives and children. Mr Sixpence was a real scrounger and he expected his family members to act likewise.

With all the money he had, he did not even open a bank account since he believed they took money in the form of interest. Every penny counted to him. Loose change was put in a canvas bag and tied around his waist. His canvas bag went everywhere with him even to his bedroom. Mr Sixpence had a very ridiculous way of living. He was actually mad.

He had only fifty-five cups of tea and a few plates as his family had to eat in turns and also had to avoid wasting water and soap by doing lots of washing. The other crucial point was that all the washing i.e. dinner ware and clothing had to be done once weekly. If not they had to lick clean the plates or tea cups. Talk up food and hygiene. One thing his family or neighbours forgot to tell him was that being unhygienic was more costly as it caused a lot of sicknesses which in turn needed lots of cash spending by way of doctor's fees and medication.

CHAPTER TWO

One day two Policemen paid a visit to Mr Sixpence's house. Two of Mr Sixpence's sons had pinched car batteries from the City garage and Mr Sixpence was using them for his radio as there was no electricity in his house. They used candles at night and fire wood for cooking.

Using their search warrant the Policemen searched his house and found the stolen items. As the children were under age, they were not arrested. Mr Sixpence deliberately sent his under aged children to do the stealing as he very well knew they would never be arrested. His young children were also trained to steal farm produces which Mr Sixpence and his wives used to prepare meals. His own farm produces would be sold at the City Grain Marketing Board.

At his farm, the Sixpence family went to bed as early as they had no lights but the younger ones were woken up at midnight so they could go and steal food from neighbours' farms. Only one child per every ten of Mr Sixpence's offsprings attended school. The one attending school would then bring his/her homework home and teach the other nine. He always reminded his children that he could not afford to pay for their school fees let alone school uniforms.

While the other children were doing the academic side, the ones left at home would take lessons on tricks of how to save money and also how to steal without being caught. The older children would be forced to steal and at the same time make it a point to be seen and then not resist being arrested. When arrested and taken to the court they had to plead guilty so they could go to prison where they would live freely i.e. free food and free accommodation.

His wives were never allowed to just sit at home and do nothing.

CHAPTER THREE

"Why did that Casino owner not pay you for your services?" Mr Sixpence was asking his youngest wife.

"Because he said that he preferred to have fun with your beautiful daughter, Fatima. Do you know what he also said? He actually opened his mouth and said that my two small breasts put him off. Please I beg do not send me to him again. He humiliated me and I felt it" replied Mr Sixpence's youngest wife almost in tears. She was well aware the consequences she would suffer by not bringing any income into the house. As it was not her fault that she had not been paid for her services, Mr Sixpence did not give her a hiding.

Because of that particular incident which had not brought him any money at all, Mr Sixpence thought it was wise to groom his better halves. He called for an urgent meeting. "Here is what I am going to teach you today – as from tomorrow onwards, my beautiful daughters will take over the jobs of entertaining rich men. Don't you ever get the idea that you are going to sit at home doing nothing because you are to go on long trips. I will explain later what we have to do. I have lost a good £100 (one hundred pounds through Petita, my youngest darling. Please may someone explain to me why on Earth Petita failed to please a man. My eldest wife gave you plenty of lessons on how to turn a man on. As long as you are married to me you do as I say and never ever forget this, you contribute towards an expenses. Nothing is for free in this house. It's only the sun which is for free and I have never seen or heard of anyone eating the sun. Do you get what I am trying to say? I am very disappointed in you Petita".

Petita's punishment was to clean all the bedrooms his youngest wives had been using to sell their bodies.

Soon after the meeting with his wives, Angela the eldest wife was asked to choose eight beautiful daughters from his ninety nine and also train them how to entertain men for money.

The rest of Mr Sixpence's bedrooms were given to tenants who paid exorbitant prices for rental purposes.

As Mr Sixpence was still angry with his wife, Petita, he asked her to get in touch with the Casino owner and invite him to come back and spend some time with his daughter, Patricia. Petita had to pay £5 (five pounds) for making the call. On arrival, the rich Casino owner was introduced to Patricia and Mr Sixpence was so overjoyed at getting his one hundred pounds back.

"It's not as if I owed your father the one hundred pounds. I have missed an important business appointment because of your father's insanity or maybe you could call it greed for money. What was so urgent about me meeting you? I do not regret though because you are very nice and pretty" said the rich business man.

"You should know my dad by now – his entire vocabulary is filled with the word money. Please do come back tomorrow" confirmed a satisfied Patricia.

"You are no different from our dad are you? What, do you think money grows on trees? If I don't work I won't be able to pay you. You don't want to spend money but you expect other people to spend their every penny. Get next to your self!" he gave her a kiss on the forehead and left. The only thing that scared people was that Mr Sixpence was a member of the dreaded Mafia. Anyone crossing his path expected to either be shot dead or face the vandalism of their properties.

As soon as he got to his office, the Casino owner received a call from Mr Sixpence, "Why did you make my daughter cry? I give you exactly twenty minutes to come back and apologise to her otherwise build a wall around your Casino because it's gonna be attacked tonight"

"Are you blackmailing me? How on Earth do you expect me to make love when I am in a bad mood? Do you like use your intestines for thinking? I am very human and I also have feelings. When I feel better I will call your daughter and see her. Patricia is a very pretty and nice person but you have taught her all the bad habits. Okay tell her I will be there in half an hour" the Casino owner said.

"Do remember to give me five pounds for this call I made to you" Mr Sixpence told his illegal son-in-law.

"Hey, you made the call. I don't remember asking you to phone me. Sixpence you are sick. Ask your wives to get a psychiatrist for you. Listen, you witch, I will pay you fifty pounds instead. I am human and I behave like one. When you die take all the money with you to hell" and he put down the receiver on him.

As agreed the Casino owner revisited the horrible Mr Sixpence's farm and went straight to Patricia's bedroom.

Instead of paying Patricia the normal charge of one hundred pounds per session, he paid her five hundred. This man was filthy rich and Mr Sixpence was really expecting him to marry his daughter, Patricia.

Mr Sixpence introduced new laws and these were; each time the lovers came to his home for entertainment, they had to bring expensive dresses for their female entertainment.

A boutique had been opened in the City centre for these dresses. Her daughters were not to wear the expensive clothes but take them instead to the boutique shop for sale. Mr Sixpence was pleased with his eight daughters because they were making more money than what his own wives had been making.

It later came to light what the eight failure wives had to do. All they had to do was take long trips to other towns were they were not known and beg money by pretending to be blind. Each chose a it and was stationed there. They would only be allowed back home after raising five hundred pounds or more.

When the naughty ones came back home faking sickness, Mr Sixpence would send their own children instead. Mr Sixpence always made it a point to deduct money for travelling expenses from his wives each time he fetched them. In his own mind Mr Sixpence had this idea that women were stupid or they had quarter brains. His wives were warned that they were free to leave him on the understanding that they left their children behind. People thought that was the reason his wives stayed married to him.

"Hey you smelly, what are you doing here this time of the day? Aren't you supposed to be out there in the pubs helping your brothers pick lost coins? I told you that you have to be in the pubs before the cleaners arrive so you can pick all the change dropped by drunkards. Why are you stubborn?" asked Mr Sixpence.

"Dad I smell because I have not had a bath for the past six months. Don't call me smelly because all the kids at school are laughing at me" replied his son.

"Whose fault is it then if you do not like to wash your own body? You are a pig that's all and no different to your mother. I told you that if you need a bath daily, you have to use neighbours' water. I do not believe in wasting water and having to pay large sums of money for the bills. By the way, how can I pay water bills if you don't steal? Use your brains okay! I don't have to do the thinking for you all" replied Mr Sixpence who never wanted to be blamed for anything.

"I came back because I was feeling hungry" his son carried on explaining.

"Believe me my son, you are safer dead if you do not work. If you listen to every word I say, you should not be feeling hungry. I said steal food. Do you want me to spell the word *steal* for you? Think and be like me, you own father. Never make it a point in your life to spend your own money. Be like the Japanese – why do something when somebody else can do it for you? I saw the Mcdonalds leave in their car a few minutes ago. Here take this hanger and follow me and I will show you how to open doors.

Once you get inside the house, go straight into their kitchen and steal as much food as you can. I will wait outside looking out for anyone coming" Mr Sixpence went to their neighbour's house and emptied their fridge.

"That was easy wasn't it? Make sure you just eat a slice of bread. You should leave the rest for your brothers and some for the rest of the week" with this Mr Sixpence left his son and went on to take a shower. He always had a bath daily but only when his family were not around.

The week before, his sons had raised two hundred and thirty pounds while coin hunting and this had been their highest that year. It could have been because it was Christmas time and bonus time where people got a thirteenth cheque.

CHAPTER THREE

One fine summer day, Mr Sixpence paid a visit to the main prison where his five teenage sons were being held in custody over theft allegations.

The judge and the jury were failing to make head or tail of this particular issue because from the moment these boys were caught stealing, they had made it easy for the policemen to arrest them. The Sixpence boys had been behaving like that for the past eight years.

The judge was fed up with seeing Mr Sixpence's sons as she had been dealing with their theft cases since they were about fourteen and now they were in their twenties and still acting very silly. Several times in the past they had been sent for rehabilitation and to jails for the juveniles but it seems it was ineffective.

Each time their rich father was asked to pay bail, he refused and people failed to understand why.

Before taking them for trial, the judge asked the policemen who had arrested them to carry out investigations on why they were always punished but never seemed to change their behaviours.

An undercover policeman visited the boys' farm and went to hire one of the daughters for fun. He paid her well and immediately he became a family friend. The Sixpences always made friends with the rich. The undercover policemen had gone posing as an ambassador of the northern country.

During his many visits to the Sixpences' farm, the undercover guy began to slowly understand the funny side of the notorious sons of Mr Sixpence. As the five sons were considered dull by their father, Mr Sixpence thought it best to get them to be thieves and after stealing, they had to wait for the policemen to arrest them. Eventually they had to end up in the prison cells where they enjoyed free everything and by so doing they would save their father's money.

Day of the court arrived but Mr Sixpence was not aware of the judge's plans.

"All rise" said the court attendant.

Everybody in that court house arose and when the judge sat down, they all sat down.

"First case: Mr Sixpence's five sons versus Timo wholesalers" said the court attendant as he handed their files to the judge.

The five sons were sent to the witness box one after the other. When asked any questions, they all gave similar answers like parrots.

The jury who had been told the history behind the notorious five were cautioned not to find them guilty.

When passing his sentence, the judge sent the big man himself, Mr Sixpence to six months in prison instead. Mr Sixpence was also asked to repay all that his five stupid sons had stolen. The judge told Mr Sixpence that the social services would be involved in the welfare of his children and that included checking that they had more than two meals a day and that they were to be enrolled into a college for educational purposes. Mr Sixpence was informed under Chapter 999 of the book of the court of law in Zabhera, that his farm faced being taken by the law and sold for the purposes of maintaining his family.

That was the last the local court saw of those five boys as Mr Sixpence did not want the police in his life as they would end up discovering a lot about his dubious behaviour.

As if he had not been cautioned enough, Mr Sixpence came out of prison and went straight to his five stupid sons and gave them new tasks. He kept his motto that none of his members had to eat for free or live for free either. The five useless boys were ordered by their father to find wooden boxes and remove all nails from them as they were going to be used to hold newly born babies' nappies instead of pins.

Their other task was to dig a big pit in their father's bedroom floor which was going to be used as a safe for keeping heir money and all their valuables.

Mr Sixpence never set his foot in any Commercial bank. Reasons given were that he hated their interest charges and on top of that it proved to be a waste of money travelling to and from the city for the purposes of withdrawing or depositing cash.

The notorious five were beaten daily each time they had meals at their own father's house. They were advised to wander around the village in search for stray dogs. In time of need, they used these dogs as meat. As he never fed them, these dogs would soon die and then his sons had the job of skinning them and once cleaned, they would be dried by putting the meat on the roof tops.

There was no cooker in his house and no fridge either as Mr Sixpence did not feel like paying any bills using his own money.

"You five witches, I want you to take turns in getting up at midnight and stealing water from next door neighbours.

You can do this by connecting our hose pipe to their taps and then water our gardens. All you have to worry about is making sure that you are not caught" Mr Sixpence was still mad with his five sons for not bringing some kind of income to help with the food expenses. This time, thank GOD for that intelligent judge, Mr Sixpence did not want them caught.

CHAPTER FIVE

One fine day Sikimo paid a visit to the nearby village where her best friend lived. Sikimo was one of Mr Sixpence's many wives.

On arrival to her friend's house, she was offered a free cup of tea. The Sixpences always enjoyed visiting people as they ate freely and at the same time saved their own food at home.

As she sat on one of the sofas enjoying the freshly brewed tea her friend had made, she asked a very funny question. "Did anyone die this week? It's been over two weeks since we had the last funeral" she asked.

"Do I look like an undertaker? How the hell am I supposed to keep track of the dead or dying people?" came the reply from her surprised friend.

The friend was under the impression that Sikimo had paid her a social visit.

According to the Sixpence family, Sikimo, one of his wives had the job of locating funerals so the entire family would attend and eat free food.

On the other hand, his other wife, Clara had the duty of locating weddings so the Sixpences Could gate crash and enjoy free meals. Invited or uninvited, they never missed those special occasions.

After recovering from the shock of realising the real purpose of Sikimo's visit, the friend informed her that there was a woman two doors from where she lived who had been given three days to live by her doctors.

Without finishing her free up of tea, Sikimo quickly bade farewell to her friend and went to tell her husband of her new discovery.

On hearing the good news, Sixpence hugged his wife Sikimo and they started making preparations to attend the funeral which was not yet there.

Fortunately enough for the Sixpences, that poor patient died that very same evening and they all went to join the rest of the neighbours at the woman's house as was the custom in their village.

Mr Sixpence always enjoyed being at the receiving end in his entire life.

This time luck was on their side as just before the one they were mourning was buried, two more people died in the very same vicinity. That meant they had a good three weeks away from their own home and they really saved money and they were also pleased with themselves.

One Easter holiday, a really funny thing happened at a wedding Mr Sixpence and his entire family attended.

Mr Sixpence's tribe were sent invitation cards which invited all including their dogs.

The children were reminded to carry with them empty plastic bags so they could bring back left over food.

"There is no need to change into new clothes. Remember what I always tell you – the Sixpences will wear clothes until they are worn out. Why not belike me? I change clothes Christmas time only. Does anyone pay you money for wearing clean clothes? I see no reason for wasting my precious water washing your smelly clothes. Unless you wives of mine are looking for new husbands. If not, wear the same clothes for the whole year because I love you for who you are. You bring money into my house and that's all I care for, understand!" exclaimed Sixpence as he banged the table with his fist.

They left their home hours before the wedding was supposed to take place. They walked for a good four hours. They managed to get the front seats as per the big boss's wish. Other people started arriving in their posh cars but Mr Sixpence never used his car. This particular car that he bought over twenty years back has a mileage of eleven miles only. The longest journey it had made was from his garage at home where it was kept to the main gate only when he was testing the engine.

Mr Sixpence was scared to use his car because he did not want to incur expenses in case of an accident. Each time his family members planned a journey, they had to hitch hike kind neighbours' cars. Mr Sixpence taught his family to respect everyone especially the well to do by calling them auntie or uncle. Asked why, he explained "if people think you are relative they will automatically find it easy to give you food or a free ride. It's all about mind games. Have you ever seen me annoying a rich person? No, it doesn't work like that. I never bite the hand that feeds me. I only hit you my family because you never have money".

"Dad, I think you are evil!" exclaimed one of his daughters who had a big mouth like her dad and who never cared for other people's feelings.

Back to the story about the wedding. The wedding was supposed to commence at two in the afternoon but by three the bride had not yet arrived.

News soon arrived that she and the people she was travelling with had had a nasty head on collision accident and all five of them had died on the spot. How could the ceremony go ahead without the bride and groom? It had to be cancelled.

After the announcement of the cancellation of the wedding, Mr Sixpence got very furious. He started shouting, "I am going to sue the person who sent me the invitation card. I used my own calculator to discover that spending two days at this wedding was going to save me about forty pounds. Now look the expense I am going to face!"

Sikimo rose up and said, "Hey, it's nobody's fault that the bride and groom are dead and stop acting as if you are the one who bought the food".

"By the way, Mr Stupid, greedy Sixpence, you should be sympathising with the family of the dead and the others who lost their loved ones. You are very selfish. Your love of money is blinding you so much you cannot see sense. By all means please remove your carcase from here and do not leave your tribe behind as we have better things to worry about" said the bridegroom's father.

"I am seeing my solicitor tomorrow and expect a letter from him for a refund of all the money I am supposed to have saved. You people are very evil. No wonder Russia manufacture ammunition to kill you and animals just need a small poisoned dart. Check on the internet for the submarines and guns and bullets used to blow your heads off. I hate you all and I hope you all die soon so that I can attend your funerals" carried on mean Mr Sixpence as he summoned his family to start another four hour journey back home. The journey back home took them longer as they were feeling weak from hunger. They had left their home with empty tummies expecting to eat plenty of food at the ruined wedding.

As soon as they arrived back home, Clara suddenly gave Mr Sixpence a bright idea. She made them realise that there were five people who had just died – the wedding crew.

"Listen, Clara, can I just ask you one thing? Why are you never alert? You made us walk for more than six hours and yet we could have just switched from the wedding to the funeral. Think woman think, you know how your husband hates stupidity. All of you my family we have to make a u-turn and go back to attend the five funeral. Clara, because of your carelessness, you have to divide the entire family into groups so that we have five groups attending five funerals. Had it not been for these funerals, I was going to sue them. This actually is a blessing in disguise. Instead of being away for only two days we have to be away for one whole week. Come on everybody let's take the journey back to go and bury the dead" said Mr Sixpence to his family. They took the tedious journey back to go and mourn them along with their relatives and friends.

“Do you ever think of anything else except saving money? How come you are staying on my mother’s farm with your wives and I never complain. The Creator cursed my womb but besides having everything for free, you still complain and you are never satisfied,” Angela said as she thought of her dead mother and her blind sister who was not enjoying the benefits of the farm.

Mr Sixpence spent another few days away from his own home and that sort of reduced his blood pressure.

Aids victims and cancer patients were his favourite friends and he definitely made it a point to make friends with their relatives. This was done for the simple reason he had to be invited to attend their funerals.

CHAPTER SIX

As Mr Sixpence was on his daily routines checking used or missing items in his house, he noticed that the toilet rolls had been over used.

He immediately called for a meeting with his family. He needed an explanation on why his family had wasted his toilet rolls.

"Dad, the three of us had running tummies" came a reply from one of his many daughters.

"I emphasised over and over again that you should not over eat. One meal a day is enough. How come you never listen? You are so dull and that's one of the reasons I never enrol you for school because it would be a total waste of my money" said the cruel father.

When he was complaining about wastage nobody dared voice.

"May I remind you again that we only flush our toilets once a week to save water. Have you ever seen animals flush their toilets – no because the first thing they don't have toilets. Have you ever truly seen animals getting sick because they are dirty? Should you over use my toilet rolls again, I promise you that I shan't be as nice as I am being today. Do you hear me?" he said as he left the room and banged the door behind him.

Weekends at Mr Sixpence's place were very awkward periods to spend time there. The whole family including visitors if any were expected or forced to have lay ins in bed until two in the afternoon. There were not supposed to have breakfast. Bed time was six in the evening latest as no candles were to be used.

The only ones allowed to stay awake after six in the evening were the boys watering the gardens using other people's water taps or the eight girls entertaining the rich guys.

During weekends, they only stayed awake for four and half hours a day in order to have only one meal a day.

This one meal a day also helped save Mr Sixpence's toilet rolls. The less food they consumed, the less they visited the toilet. In case there was left over food, it had to be stored away and ate the following day.

It so happened one winter that Mr Sixpence's next door neighbour was facing losing his job in the supermarket where he worked as an accountant.

He thought of going to his rich neighbour, Mr Sixpence to sell his television and radio in order to raise the sixty pounds he had taken from the cash till. He had been warned by one of the clerks that the firm auditors would be visiting his company in two days' time.

To the stranded neighbour's surprise, Mr Sixpence refused to buy the items although he he did not own a television set neither a radio.

"Please, help me save my job" said his friend.

"Listen you pervert, all your money goes on those expensive cars you show around in the village. I am not responsible for your problems and don't keep bothering me. Look at me, I have a car which I never use. My wives and my own flesh and blood pay for everything they use in my house. You are sick because you allow that fat wife of yours to stay at home all day long doing nothing. Why did you hire a nanny for? Surely your wife can cook and look after her on children, can't she? Those extra rooms in your big house should be rented out at a profit. My sixteen wives only use two bedrooms – eight per room. You caused your own poverty. Leave me alone! I never want dull people near me" came the rude reply from the funny Mr Sixpence.

Luckily enough for the desperate accountant, the pub owner bought the two items and paid a hundred pounds for them instead of the sixty he initially needed. At least he had secured his job.

It so happened one Spring that that there were no funerals in the neighbourhood and that made Mr Sixpence panic a lot. He eagerly watched the food in his store house finishing quick and he decided to do something about it. He called some of his greedy children who te a lot and asked to start fighting amongst themselves. The twenty were to hurt each other until they bled. After fighting for a good two hours, they were so hurt that the evil father had to call ambulances.

While they were waiting for the ambulances to come, the injured crew were told to tell the hospital staff that they had been attacked by a group of thieves who wanted to steal from their farm, although there was nothing to steal as he had no furniture in his house. "Once you are admitted, stay hospitalised for as long as ever. Even if they think you have healed, they still have to take your body temperature. I shall visit you before hand and bring you salt. During their rounds to take your temperatures, put salt under your tongue a few minutes before and this will raise your body temperature again. Will you do that for your daddy my little angels? You will also be enjoying good hospital food not this crap that my sick wives prepare here. Don't forget that I don't want you back soon. Three years will do me fine" said sick Mr Sixpence.

The ambulances soon arrived and the wounded twenty were taken to the main hospital where according to their dad enjoyed the good food the hospital served and moreover it was three meals a day. Thank God for their wicked father's evil plans.

"Every little helps" he always told his family.

In the thirtieth year as a married polygamist, Mr Sixpence had saved about five hundred thousand pounds which he kept in his underground safe.

CHAPTER SEVEN

After Patrick and Peter, his eldest children who were born twins finished their high school studies, their father asked them to find jobs in hotels.

People always believed that Mr Sixpence's rituals involved starving his family.

Both Patrick and Peter qualified to work in offices and earn more money but the fact of them coming home for meals really disturbed their father.

Nobody ever won an argument with Mr Sixpence especially the ones concerning food issues. Even food bought by any member of his family belonged to him. "The point is, when you are a chef in a hotel, you eat anytime you feel like from breakfast to supper. By the time you come home after work, you will be so full you won't need to eat food from my house and also it saves me electricity and water. Listen to me my kids, if you ever decide to get office jobs, I do not want you to attend my funeral! Can you eat pen and paper? So why get a job in an office when you can work in a hotel and get free meals. Use your brains not only sometimes but all the time. Are you sure you are my flesh and blood? I am beginning to think your mother mucked about with my cousin Elliot because he surely had no brains. When you get your first wages, please pay the doctor so we can have DNA tests!" Mr Sixpence kept screaming at his twins.

For the sake of peace, the twins got jobs in the city hotel which was owned by their father's friend. Everybody who knew him always wondered whether Mr Sixpence was mad, or brainless or worse still was it his love for money that made him be so impossible. Even his own family failed to understand him. People tried to reason with him but they could never manage to put sense into his head which seemed to be very thick.

Fed up with his father's ill behaviour which seemed to get worse and not better, one of Mr Sixpence's son left his home town and went to Zoba, a country in the North side of Zibhera. He just wanted to start a new life altogether.

He did not know the language there because it was different from his mother's but he soon learnt and a few months later, he married a local native girl of Zoba.

After the little amount of money given to him by his mean father finished, he decided to start his own business. The son of a snake will always have its parents' genes and will behave like a snake.

He decided to start his own church with the hope of taking money from church members by way of offerings and tithes.

The funny thing was that Funny, Mr Sixpence's son had never set foot in any church in his entire life. Funny had small ideas which he had heard from his grandfather who had been a church leader.

Funny and his wife moved to a posh area where rich heathens lived and hired a hall there. Many residents there joined Funny's church. Funny held fifteen minutes sermons every Sunday where he talked about nothing religious except common topics he had heard from some Christians who used to visit his home town.

At the end of each service, his wife passed a dish around and the rich church members poured lots of money. They only went to church to ease their guilty consciences. There was no bible in Funny's church. His church members were raw heathens so nothing mattered much. One Sunday morning a very nice lady from his church asked why they never sang any hymns in their church. He had almost been caught. As soon as he got home after the morning service, Funny took a book and started writing down some of the proverbs and songs his mother used to sing to him.

The following Sunday, Funny took a board and wrote his songs and taught his church members how to sing them.

Before the main church service started, he told his congregation that he had something important to tell them which he had received from his god. He asked them all to sit down and cautioned them to take heed.

Funny went to the altar and knelt down and gave his long speech which went, "After speaking to sister Maureen last Sunday, I went home and prayed for two whole days without eating. On the third day I started speaking in unknown tongues. Then came this strange voice which asked me to write all my songs in the heavenly languages. My people, from today onwards, all our hymns will be sung in heavenly languages – angels' language. Please do not ask me to interpret them because I, myself, don't know what they mean. Thank you very much ladies and gentlemen.

After that Funny wrote the songs on the board. The reality was that these songs were rhymes and proverbs from his home town and they were in his mother's language. One of them went like this;

Dzamutsana tsuro

Tsuro

Tsuro nembwa (2)

Interpreted the song meant the hare and the dog are attacking each other and chasing each other.

His church members were overjoyed to receive messages from heaven. During that wonderful sermon, all church members gave more than hundred pounds each. Funny got very popular and opened churches in other countries except his own. Funny hated sick people joining his church because he did not know how to pray to the Creator and ask for their healing.

His churches were full of the rich people only. In order to please them, he made sure he did not take too much of their time as they needed to go back to their homes and businesses or games. Like his father, Funny was getting richer and richer without using his own money.

One day, after hearing on the local news about his son's success, Mr Sixpence thought of paying him a visit. Mr Sixpence wanted to trick his son into keeping his money for him in his own underground safe which was in his bedroom.

Mr Sixpence took with him his youngest wife who was very jealousy of Funny and his mother. On arrival, they were introduced to most of Funny's church members.

Luckily enough, Mr Sixpence's wife had been born and bred in that country and had left at the age of eighteen fleeing domestic violence from her step father who wanted to marry her after the death of her mother. After hearing the Funny's church choir sing, she raised her hand in the middle of service and started exposing Funny. She explained to the church members that the hymns they were singing were not Biblical. Funny's aunt begged the church members to be reimbursed but being they were filthy rich people they refused to be refunded. After that incident, Funny's churches were all closed down and he was cautioned never to repeat the same sins again.

Funny and his father never saw eye to eye again. Through this, Mr Sixpence lost his son's love and trust.

Since he had failed to get money from Funny, Mr Sixpence was so furious that when he got home, he ordered eight of his wives to go and get jobs in the local shops and supermarkets and work as cleaners.

Their duty was to concentrate more on the food thrown away by the supermarkets at the end of each business day. Even Angela, who was now in her late seventies secured herself a job as a cleaner and acted like wise, bringing not so clean food back home. One of his wife did not join them because her husband had a special job for her which she was soon to know.

The faking blind ones were still bringing lots of money home while the cleaners were bringing wages and food daily – just the way Mr Sixpence wanted it.

He always wore a big smile on his face every time he took his family's earnings to his safe. Mr Sixpence's himself was self-employed and his job was to check stock of the food and counting the money earned by his wives and kids. The wives who were cleaners really pleased him and they got extra affection from him each time they brought food home. Mr Sixpence put a board a board in his kitchen which read: NO NEED WASTING MONEY DOING SHOPPING WHEN YOU CAN GET FOOD FREE!

CHAPTER EIGHT

Biggie, was the only son who never feared his father and hence he had no need of taking heed to anything he said.

When he needed anything, he demanded from his dad and if it wasn't given to him, he would throw stones at him. The funny part about these two was that they were very every close.

All his wives begged Mr Sixpence to punish his son but Mr Sixpence had a soft spot for Biggie. Biggie was the apple of his eye. It might have been for the fact that Biggie was impossible like his dad and he resembled him both in deeds and body build.

Mr Sixpence never bought shoes for any of his tribe but as for Biggie, he always bought him an expensive pair of shoes each time the old pair wore out. Each time Biggie wanted his dad to do anything for him, he would threaten to set fire to the whole farm. One festive season, Biggie's friend got a pair of the latest model shoes so Biggie asked his dad to buy him a pair similar to the ones his friend owned.

Since that particular pair of shoes had cost him a fortune and a half, Mr Sixpence as usual had to give his son a big lecture before giving him his shoes. Mr Sixpence called Biggie and said to him, "In case you are walking in the bush or forest or any rough parts, make sure you remove your shoes. By so doing, you will be protecting your shoes from small stones, animal poo and any other damages. Remember, it costs money to repair shoes".

One day Biggie was taking walks with his best friend and they decided to take a short cut via the forest. The path was not so bad as it was mainly sand so Biggie saw no point in removing his new pair of shoes.

After walking for some time Biggie noticed something which looked like a piece of chocolate cake. He picked a bit with his finger an after tasting it, he discovered that it was wild animal dung. Biggie had had lots of training from his family that they had to watch out for valuables each time they went anywhere. To his friend's surprise, Biggie said, "At least I did not step on it with my new pair of shoes". Biggie was extra relieved that his expensive pair of shoes was safe from damage. The idea of having to wash them or clean them using chemicals would have killed his dad. All the way back home though he was feeling sick.

As soon as he got home Biggie vomited and was being sick all over the kitchen floor. Much to everyone's surprise, Mr Sixpence ordered Biggie's mother to carefully fetch the vomits from the floor and save it for Biggie to eat later.

As Biggie's mother was busy cleaning the smelly stuff, Mr Sixpence opened his mouth and said, "Dogs eat their vomit and nobody ever sees them getting sick never mind dying. I, personally see no reason why it should be a big deal eating our own vomits. It's just the same food you ate isn't it?"

Within the first six days of Mr Sixpence's twins working in a hotel, their father demanded they be introduced to the daughters of the rich hotel owner. Although the daughters were a good twenty two years older than Patrick and Peter, Mr Sixpence advised his twins to get to know them better with the hope of eventually marrying them. These two daughters were also twins but very loose women. They happened to have shares in their father's businesses and their father's will left his entire fortune to them.

Mr Sixpence, as usual gave lectures to his twins by saying, "You know what, my children, it is always good to marry a rich woman. It does not matter whether you love them or not. The bottom line is winning their love first then marrying them and filing for divorce after a short period then divide their riches with them. At your age, you can play this game with more than twenty rich woman and end up multi billionaires. Should you decide to stay married to them for life, you still live a luxurious life your whole life but the best is to keep divorcing and remarrying a new rich wife. That way you accumulate the riches of each of your exs".

The marriages were arranged and since Patrick and Peter were twins and the brides twins too, they wedded on the same day. Exactly a year after the two pairs of twins married, the father of the wives died. Patrick and Peter were asked to take over the business by their wives. Luckily enough for them all, they never divorced.

Being a father of many children, Mr Sixpence was still finding it hard to feed his family. He called for another meeting and came up with some very crazy ideas which he thought would bring money into his household.

The plans included sending some of his daughters to act as prostitutes but not in his house. The girls had to go to hotels where the rich met, pretend to drink but not get drunk and then after the pubs or hotels closed for the day, they each followed their rich boyfriends to their homes for the night.

As they would be leaving the hotels or pubs with their picks for the day, their brothers' job was to follow behind and hide outside while their sisters entered the house with their victims. They would have individual affairs of course. Each sister was to be followed by one or two of their brothers and that depended on the physique of the boy friend.

During the time the couples would be having fun inside the house, the wicked sister would give a sign to the waiting brothers by switching off the lights.

The brother or brothers would then enter and rob the house. If the lover was stupid or too drunk, he would be forced to give the combination code for his safe. Should it happen that during these robberies, the victim retaliates, he would be got rid of.

Many business people were either beaten or killed and then buried in unmarked graves.

The furniture stolen from these house beak-ins were sold in a second hand furniture shop which Mr Sixpence had opened specifically for that. Some silly business men repurchased goods that had been stolen from their own homes.

CHAPTER NINE

Bertha, Mr Sixpence's wife, who spent more time with him than the rest of his wives was reported missing after she had left home with the intention of visiting her mom. Her mom lived in another town.

Unbeknown to everyone, Mr Sixpence had planned with Bertha that she disappear and then be pronounced dead after a few months' search. The whole idea was for Mr Sixpence to claim money from the Insurance people over Bertha's life policy where the coin man was beneficiary.

It was unlike Betha to visit her mom and pay a social visit because Mr Sixpence never paid travelling expenses for anybody. Instead, his wives'relatives had to do the visiting and at the same time bring their own blankets and food. The ones who owned big cars had to bring their own beds and sofas. Most brought small stools with them. If not, they had to expect a bill from Mr Sixpence for costs incurred. People wondered why Bertha had suddenly decided to visit her own mother for the first time in her married life. That kind of behaviour by Bertha raised a lot of questions in people's minds especially the police and close relatives who knew the Sixpences well.

Mr Sixpence was cross questions at the local police station but he maintained his innocence all the time. After searching for eight months, Bertha was declared dead.

After receiving a cheque from the Insurance company, Mr Sixpence went and cashed the whole three hundred thousand pounds from the bank and hid it in his safe where he kept all his treasures.

The other crucial thing was that Bertha was two months pregnant during the time of her disappearance. Bertha had not told her husband about her pregnancy for the obvious reason she felt if it was a boy, her husband would not be very pleased with her. She had been her husband's favourite for the simple reason that all her children were girls and six of them were the loose ones entertaining rich men in his house. Bertha was so determined that if her baby came out a boy, she was going to secretly ask her mom to raise the kid. It was better than being told off by her husband as if it took one person to make babies.

Mr Sixpence had made plans with her that he would be visiting her every so often. Since it was illegal for Mr Sixpence to tell the truth, he never visited her. Out of sight and out of mind. As Mr Sixpence never carried out his promises, Bertha started to panic as she was running out of food and the baby needed proper food and accommodation. By the way according to her fears, Bertha gave birth to a baby boy.

Alone in the middle of the forest where she lived alone with her son and faced with hunger and death, Bertha started recalling the day she had left home and the promises her husband had made to her. Mr Sixpence had arranged with her that he was going to bring some of the proceeds of her life policy and build her a palace where he would spend six months with her every year.

Being a woman, Bertha got fed up of waiting in vain and decided to go back to her husband and face the consequences. The wooden house she had built for herself was being blown by the strong winds and she was tired or repairing it.

When her son was turning five, Bertha gave him lessons on how to hunt and catch small animals like squirrels or mice. Twoboy, Bertha's son was very lazy but intelligent just like his father. He really was a chip off the old block. Bertha had to do everything for him.

Bertha kept battling in her mind that although she wanted to go back home, it was proving impossible because she hardly remembered her way home as she had lived there for long.

While he was growing up, Twoboy learnt all he needed to know about his own family who he was so eager to meet.

One day, on his seventh birthday, Twoboy's mom, Bertha fell off a hill while chasing a rabbit which she intended to use in celebrating his birthday. She bled heavily and it seems she was losing consciousness. Twoboy pulled his injured mother to their small hut, lit a fire for her and made plans to go find his family.

It took Twoboy a good six days to find his family's home. He was met by Mr Sixpence who was very surprised to hear Twoboy's strange story.

"Why was she hunting when I told her to wait for me as I was coming there myself to sort things out?" asked Mr Sixpence who never took a blame for his sick behaviour.

"Dad it's more than seven years since my mother left here. How can you ask a silly question like that?" said Twoboy who had already started to dislike his own dad.

"Tell you what son, this has to remain a secret between the two of us. You have to go back before people see you and I promise to come after you within the next few days. Your mother's case is a police issue and if caught here alive, I will be arrested" Mr Sixpence said as he walked towards his store house where he knew passer bys would not see Twoboy. If people saw Bertha's son, they would put two and two together and come up with a dangerous answer.

"Okay dad" said Twoboy eyeing one mule and a calf which he was planning to steal and take with him on his way back home. He also said, "I will wait until dark and then leave". Twoboy stayed in the storehouse until evening.

At dusk, Twoboy killed the calf and rode on the mule and took the long journey back to his supposed to be dying mother. He got back in time to see his mother still alive but at the point of death. He quickly prepared a meal and fed her but Bertha had lost so much blood she died three weeks later.

The seven year old dug a hole and buried his one and only friend, his mother. Twoboy swore he was going to take revenge for what his dad had made her mother pass through.

After burying his mother single handily, Twoboy took another trip back to his father's mansion.

On arrival, Twoboy was introduced as Mr Sixpence's nephew.

After settling in with his family, Twoboy demanded that his father enrol him into a very expensive school. Twoboy very well knew that his dad had been paid lots of money by way of faking his mother, Bertha's death.

When Mr Sixpence refused to take Twoboy to the school of his choice, the naughty boy went straight to the police and spilt the beans. Mr Sixpence was surprised to see two police vans drive into his farm with Twoboy sitting in front in one of the vans.

"We are here to arrest you under suspicion of the murder of your wife, Bertha and fraud of three hundred thousand pounds. You may remain silent because whatever you say will be used as evidence in the court of law" said one of the officers as he handcuffed Mr Sixpence. He pushed him to the back of the police van and drove to the police station.

During questioning, Mr Sixpence continually denied that Twoboy was his son. DNA samples were taken from Mr Sixpence and his carbon copy. Unfortunately the results came back positive.

Mr Sixpence remained under police custody as some of the policemen drove to the place where Bertha had been buried by her seven year old son. True to Twoboy's statements, Bertha's body was found and taken back to the farm for a decent burial.

While the police officers and Central Intelligent officers were carrying out further investigations pending Mr Sixpence's trial, Angela, the eldest wife, made arrangements for Bertha's funeral to be held at the farm.

Bertha's funeral was held in the absence of Mr Sixpence. Let's face it, he wasn't needed anyway – or was he after all he was the one who had caused the death.

Since Mr Sixpence's cash was kept and lock and key, his children had to wander around the village and surrounding areas requesting people to bring their own food not forgetting toilet rolls.

As the mourners started arriving, some of Mr Sixpence's offsprings sat at the gate checking to see if each and everyone had brought with them all the food and toiletries needed to be used during their short stay at the farm. The ones who forgot were sent back to their homes.

All went according to plan and Twoboy smiled as he watched the lifeless body of his mother being finally laid to rest in a dignified way.

CHAPTER TEN

Two days after Bertha's funeral, Mr Sixpence was sentenced to eighteen months in prison. His solicitor fought hard to have him freed from being charged of the death of Bertha. As he had not actually killed Bertha, Mr Sixpence was cleared of her death but served eighteen months for fraud. The punishment never raised his blood pressure as Mr Sixpence had always prayed for any opportunity to have free food and free accommodation. Mr Sixpence posted his safe keys to his oldest wife, Angela. The keys were accompanied with a letter which read; '*Hi, I have given you these keys. Every Monday, go and collect the cheques from the welfare offices, cash them and hide the money in my safe.'*

Angela knew better than to spend a penny of that money. But as hunger struck, Angela summoned eleven of her husband's children and made plans to use some of the money for income generating projects and then quickly replace all the money before her husband got back home from prison. While the cat was away, the mice surely played with their tails waggling in the air.

Using the borrowed money before approval of the owner, the Sixpence family bought a piece of land which was situated on the outskirts of the city centre and built a crematorium, a funeral parlour and a grave yard. The main reason behind was for the boys to steal gold teeth belonging to the deceased and steal coffins the same night, the occupants were buried.

Four of the sons were employed as grave diggers. Most families bought the same coffin more than twice to bury their family members, ignorantly of course. Money was coming in fast.

In the absence of their father, the Sixpences were now enjoying three meals a day. Birthdays were now being celebrated freely. The last day they had seen their father was the day he was sentenced and then a week later. A week into his sentence, the members of his family who visited him were given a lecture. He said, "You miserable offenders! Tell me where you will get the money to pay for your transport because I don't want you using my welfare money. Believe me I will be fine. The government is stupid enough not to charge me rent and cost of living. I am having three meals a day and I sleep on a bed with clean linen which is changed on a daily basis. If the government is silly enough not to charge me for my expenditure, why should you want to spend my money visiting me? I also have bodyguards twenty four hours a day. I am safer than you. The next time I want to see you, is the day I leave this place. The queen of Spain has body guards 24/7 and I have body guards 24/7 also. If you use your loaf you can make your enemies your slaves. The innocent victims world wide pay their way in life for everything and me and my mates here, we don't buy milk, bread, meat or even clothes so why should you worry about me? In fact it should be the other way round – I should be worrying about you."

At this point in time, with these evil words, his family and friends lost interest in him. Nobody knew how to please Mr Sixpence. One of Mr Sixpence's parents' neighbours had said jokingly, "The mother of Mr Sixpence had had an affair with a one pound coin and Mr Sixpence had been the product of that funny union". Everything about him was money and eventually people got fed up with him. He had no time to socialise or entertain friends never mind his own wives.

The business of burying the dead in dubious ways was blossoming and Angela and her crew enjoyed spending the profits from it. They only spent the profit and the rest of the money was replaced bit by bit and securely kept under lock and key.

CHAPTER ELEVEN

Bertha's son, Twoboy was now getting used to his father's wives and step brothers and sisters. The odd thing was he still missed his mother although she was now buried nearby. The other thing was Twoboy missed his birthplace and memories of him and his mother living there kept haunting him. It got to a point were he was having nightmares and he finally decided to confide in one of his brothers.

"Hey Frank, there is something bothering me and it's now getting to a stage where I feel if I don't do something about it, I will definitely lose my mind".

"What is it exactly?" asked Frank.

"This might sound funny but the truth is I miss the woods where I was born and my mother's things and the toys she made for me. It's like something in me keeps drawing me there. I just feel I have to go there. I know my mother is now buried here but the memories of that place keeps tormenting me. Tell me, how do I overcome this?" replied Twoboy.

"Listen since the coin is not here – you and me will make some plans and go there just to satisfy your curiosity," came the answer from Frank.

"Thank you for that thought but the problem is what are we going to eat? I am planning to spend a week or so. I also made friends with seven monkeys and three lions and I just want to see them and maybe say bye to them like officially. The times when my mother was sick, the monkeys got me fruits and some food stuffs. They were like my own family there and we got to a point where we could like read each other's mind. I just knew what they wanted and the reverse was true. I feel like I abandoned them. The first time the lions met my mother, they never ate her. I don't even know why but after my mom told me she had met some lions and they had not attacked her, I wondered. I explained to her that they were my mates and she burst into laughter." Twoboy continued telling his half brother his childhood memories.

"I was listening to the news last night at the pub and I heard them saying there was drought in that area where I used to live and that's why I had to tell you because I panicked and without water, my animal family might need me. Either I bring them here and confess to the sixpence coin or I visit them regularly to take food to them. Do we have a deal?" Twoboy was now in tears at this point and Frank hugged him and promised he would go with him.

Frank sat with his half brother for the rest of the day telling him jokes with the hope of taking his young mind from the problems that were bothering him.

Eventually, they decided to steal money from their evil father's safe and take it with them so they could build a zoo and take care of wild animals. It sounded a great idea to Twoboy but the question was how were they going to steal the money without the rest of the family knowing about it since weekly, Angela checked on the money at the same time putting some more.

Twoboy said, "There is money in that safe which is rightfully mine because my mother was tricked by my wicked dad to raise insurance money. By faking her own death, my dad got money and I have every right to take it without feeling guilty about it".

"I know you are still hurting. But everybody here is scared of dad and what he will do to anyone who tempers with his savings. Imagine how each time our big brothers get jobs and dad controls their wages. If he feels strongly about other people's money, how on earth are you going to take his money which is rightfully yours and at the same time according to his opinions rightfully his?" Frank said as he seemed to be getting more scared of the thought of stealing from his evil dad.

"Are you backing out on me? Either way, as long as you live, you will never spend that man's money. We might as well steal the money because we are all living his life and not ours. I am prepared to kill in order to get what belongs to me. In fact it's not stealing but just retrieving what belongs to me. Do we have a deal here?" asked Twoboy.

Frank suddenly came out with a very crazy idea and he said, "Angela is as tough as dad. We just have to kill her and anybody else who blocks our ways to stardom. Please I would appreciate it if you don't say anything now. You have dragged me into this against my will because I would not dare cross his path. From now on you do things my way, and for the records, I have lived longer than you on this farm and in real life. What I mean is I am older than you and I go further to say it might mean I have more life experiences than you and also you spent most of your life living in the forest and that does not give you experience with us, ordinary human beings – okay you miserable individual!"

Twoboy took a very deep breath and said, "If it wasn't for the fact that I am dying to see my animal friends, I would stage a fight with you right now because what you just said hurt my feelings."

Plans were made to steal the money that very same night.

CHAPTER TWELVE

Twoboy was asked to fetch dry firewood from the forest for the purposes of making a very special fire. Plan B was to boil gallons of water. It was suggested by mastermind Frank that while Angela was sleeping, Frank would enter her room and pour boiling water on her to silence her for good. From there, the two partners in crime had to take the keys of the safe from her waist where she kept them tied around in a leather belt which she had stolen from a clothes shop during one of her visits shoplifting in the city centre.

Since they were going to stay in a place with no shops, Frank thought it wise that they just take a small amount of money. Twoboy was so angered by that idea that he hit Frank hard on his forehead with his bare fist.

"Hey what was that for?" asked Frank.

"How dare you say stupid things like that? I am talking about my mother here! Because of her going six feet under, I have to live with grief and sadness all my life. If I was doing this deal with her right now, she would be agreeing with me in everything every inch of the way. Sixpence got lots of money through her death and I need every penny of it. Anyway why should Auntie Angela die for us to steal a small amount of money?" asked the furious Twoboy.

"Hallo! The only way to get the keys to the safe is by killing Angela. Even if we needed one pound we would still have to kill her. Please explain to me how on earth we can carry a lot of money fro this farm to wherever you want us to go?" asked Frank who was always argumentative like his dad.

"I tell you what we are going to do. We are going to steal the car from the garage and put all the money there and kiss this place goodbye. We might not even have to go to the place where you were born because the police know about it and it will be easy for dad to locate us. Remember we are committing two crimes here – one for murdering Auntie Angela and the other one for theft. By the way if you have any better idea can we hear it now as the clock is ticking and it will soon be daylight and it might seem impossible to fight about one hundred and fifty people who happen to be dad's wife and children – okay!" screamed Frank at his young half brother who to him seemed to have half brains.

"Okay, you are right. We will just steal the money we need. Since we will only need a fence around our zoo, we just take about nine hundred pounds. This will be easy to carry and we will just steal two horses from the farm next door. Any more problems with that?" asked Twoboy.

“I refuse to do any more killings. To steal horses you have to kill the owners. Listen the deal is off okay! A few more years in this farm will wipe away your memories of your birthplace. That’s it, I quit and I am going to sleep. Goodnight” said frank.

“No, no Frank. You step on my toes, and I kill you. Your father, Sixpence is in prison because of my big mouth. I phoned the police and told them everything. You walk away from me now and I will phone the police and show them all these gallons of water. I have a good reputation there because all I told them was proven correct. I say we carry on. The water has boiled already and you pour it on Angela as per our arrangements” said the cruel Twoboy.

“You are real mean like your father. While I am killing your innocent Auntie, you go and steal the two horses and I pray you are caught red handed so the police will arrest you instead. Run quick before I change my mind. What’s in it for me anyway? You are a user like your father. From now on I will call you Sixpence Junior and that will be a constant reminder of how much Sixpence’s blood runs inside your veins!” Frank said while froth was coming out of his mouth. He was also shaking at the thought of killing Auntie Angela.

Twoboy went to fetch his father’s gun to use it in case of disturbances.

Within six minutes of him leaving the house, Frank heard shots and people screaming and a few minutes later Twoboy walked in with blood on his clothes.

“Hurry, hurry, I have shot the entire except the wife and I think she is phoning the police. She recognised me before she locked herself in her bedroom and the last I heard was her voice shouting, ‘come soon before the intruder attacks me!’” screamed Twoboy.

“How many people have to die for just nine hundred pounds? We might as well empty the safe and make it worth spending eternity in prison! Twoboy you are impossible. Now I understand why my father never made an effort to follow you and your dead mother. I am now suffering for her death which has got nothing to do with me. Go on hit me again and make sure I faint because right now I feel like calling the cops for me and you” cried Frank.

“The phone is locked my dear Frank ha ha ha!” said Twoboy.

“The police number is free phone – you twart” Frank said while still holding the jug he had used to kill Auntie Angela.

“No, you are wrong – our phone is an old one and Antie Angela puts a cage around it and then locks it with a very strong key.” Replied Twoboy.

“You are a proper criminal aren’t you? How do you know all these details and yet you have only been here like two minutes?” asked Frank who felt belittled by his half young brother and he carried on to say, “Are you coming or not? Okay, I admit I am very sorry but we have no time to argue. Either way we are in big trouble. The only better chance is us escaping and try and enjoy life a little bit before we are finally caught. I killed dad’s oldest wife and you wiped away entire family. So let’s go although I still can’t believe innocent blood was shed for only nine hundred pounds. Truthfully, Twoboy, I hate you so much and I am beginning to admire my father because all he lives for is other people’s money without shedding blood”

The two musketeers left for their trip to an unknown land without enough to cover their future. Frank now wished he had taken Twoboy’s advice to take all the money but since he was older, the African custom was the old are always right so he found it hard to confess that he was wrong.

After riding for hours and hours the two Sixpences finally arrived at what Twoboy called his home. Frank could hardly believe his eyes when Twoboy showed him something that looked like a dog kennel and said that was his bedroom.

“Is this what you were aching to see? This thing which looks like a dog kennel. You mean We killed so many innocent people for this? Twoboy I am going to kill you right now! Here is what I am going to do. I am going to shoot you first and then gather enough courage to shoot you because if I am still alive within the next six minutes I will lose my mind” said Frank as he prepared to shoot Twoboy.

“Listen, you potato head witch, I begged you to steal all the money because I knew we needed it but no like all African big brothers, you had to be right. I never said I had a home, I specifically told you that I wanted to visit the place where I was born” replied Twoboy and also carried on to say, “Bertha my mother slept in that cave over there while I slept in this house” said Twoboy.

“If you call this house anymore I am definitely going to shoot you!” screamed Frank as he covered his face with his hands trying not to see what was facing him.

“There are no pots, no blankets and no food – how are we going to survive in this place?” asked Frank without giving his intelligent brother time to explain himself further.

“Listen buddy, we are going to kill one horse and eat some of the meat for dinner. We are both tired and I can’t see us hunting for meat” said Twoboy very calmly as if he was saying something brilliant.

“One more word from you and I am going to shoot you and hand myself over the police and then join my father in prison where there is fine food and bedding and normal bedrooms” Frank said and took a walk around the forest.

Less than five minutes later, Frank came running very fast screaming, “The lion wants to kill me please Twoboy help me!”

Frank just got in time to hide behind his brother who seemed not to be affected by what he was seeing. Much to his surprise, Twoboy did some funny signs and the lion sat down.

“Are we agreed that I am the boss now - Harry meet Frank my brother and Frank this is Harry one of my animal friends” said Twoboy as he introduced the scared Frank to his new family members.

“Remember this, if you ever try to escape from this forest you will be eaten alive” Twoboy said that and burst into a very loud laughter.

Twoboy waited until his brother felt better and they decided to go squirrel hunting since the thought of eating a horse was scaring him.

They were fortunate enough to catch two squirrels and on their way back, Twoboy fetched some firewood. They got home safely and Twoboy thought of treating his brother by making the fire himself and roasting the squirrels himself.

Since Frank was tired and feeling uncomfortable with his new lifestyle, Twoboy thought it wise to let him sleep. They walked a few steps to the cave and Frank slept in the cave which had once belonged to Twoboy’s mom.

Twoboy sat in front of the dying fire whilst trying to figure out how both he and Frank were going to make it in their new home. After a while he started feeling sorry for his brother and after realising the risks his brother had taken to help him quench his desire to visit his birth place he promised himself that he was going to make both their lives better. Even if the police caught them, Twoboy was prepared to admit to both crimes, the killings and the theft and let his brother go free.

Twoboy shelved the criminal activities at the back of his head and went ahead planning their future minus the police.

“How long are your intestines?” asked Frank as soon as he opened his eyes after his deep long sleep.

“What kind of question is that? Nobody knows the length of their intestines except the mortuary crew. Tell me, why are you asking me a silly question like that?” asked Twoboy who was so pleased to hear his brother’s voice as he had prepared a good breakfast and was waiting for him to wake up and enjoy it.

“I want to find the answer for you by killing you and then measuring your intestines myself” replied Frank.

“Are you still mad with me? I don’t mind you killing me but the question remains how are you going to get out of this forest without me?” asked Twoboy calmly as he seemed never bothered with his brother’s mood. He carried on to say “by all means, I don’t mind you killing me but please have something to eat first because you will need lots of energy in case a lion chases you again”.

“Stop blackmailing me! I hate it when you do that. I will eat and then I will go back home because I refuse to live like this. Don’t even think you can try to convince me. I am prepared to go to prison okay” replied Frank.

Without saying a further word, the two brothers went and sat next to the fire place and enjoyed a breakfast of squirrel meat and two apples.

“Where did you get these nice apples from?” asked Frank as he bit a piece of apple.

“Promise you won’t scream at me if I tell you?” asked Twoboy who was finding it hard to prove himself less intelligent than his brother.

“Any more surprises won’t scare me because from the minute I set my bare feet in this palace of yours, everything seems like a fairy tale or in your case a demonic tale” replied Frank.

“Actually it was Bonny who brought the apples and by Bonny I mean one of my monkey friends. I took the liberty of eating most of them and left just two because I wasn’t sure whether you would eat them or not” said Twoboy.

“No problem. Thanks anyway. I guess I was hungry. I am starting to feel better after having all that meat to myself. How come you are not sharing the meat with me?” asked Frank.

“Remember we caught two squirrels and I ate mine already while you were fast asleep” Twoboy said and knew that he had managed to belittle his brother again.

“I will have more rest today and then maybe tomorrow I will help with the hunting for more food” said Frank as he realised that he was meant to comfort his young brother who seemed more affected with the surroundings as it looked as though he was wishing his mother had not died.

CHAPTER THIRTEEN

Back home at the Sixpence farm, the rest of the survivors were still panicking at the terrible death of Angela. The boiling water which had killed her had caused her skin to shrink. It was such a horrible sight. The police were called and they took finger prints and took statements. Everyone was also so surprised to learn that the entire family living next door except one had been shot dead.

The police needed no evidence as it was obvious that the two missing brothers had done the work. The only problem was to try and locate their whereabouts.

Unfortunately, before the police had been called, five of Sixpence's sons had used the keys left by Frank to open the safe and steal some money for their own personal greed. They had overhead Frank and Twoboy's conversation on how to steal money and start a project in the forest. As they were aware of the fact that Frank had been cowardice enough to kill and steal peanuts, they themselves stole over one hundred thousand pounds.

Shelly was called to the funeral of her favourite aunt and made all the arrangements for her burial. Shelly's blind mother also came to pay her tribute to her sister.

After Angela's funeral, Shelly begged her mother for both of them to stay on the farm which belonged to her late grandmother. While Shelley was preparing to take over legally, her worst enemy was released from prison. The ugly coin was back. Sixpence was back to cause more heartaches to his family and the neighbours.

"Why didn't he just die in prison?" asked Shelly as she was ironing her blouse which she was going to wear on her trip to the lawyers.

"Can somebody please boil some water and pour it on Mr Sixpence because his presence makes me sick. I wish Frank was here as he could have just killed him" said one of his young wives.

As they were busy talking about him, a police car suddenly pulled in the drive way and the coin came out and entered the house.

"How come you are not so keen to see me? Did any of you ever miss me?" asked Mr Sixpence.

“Excuse me, Mister, I think you are the one who actually begged us not to visit you. Right now we do not know what to do because it so happens that whatever action we take, it always makes you unhappy. There is too many hands here to hug you. All we are waiting for is for you to give us a green light” replied Shelley.

“You are Shelley aren’t you and what the hell are you doing on my farm?” asked the wicked Sixpence coin. Everybody who knew Mr Sixpence always felt better to refer him as the coin because that clearly made them realise his true identity. It was all about money with Mr Sixpence. Nothing else mattered to him except the mention of money and how he could lay his filthy hands on it.

“How dare you have the guts to ask me what I am doing here? It so happens that this so called farm of yours belongs to my mother. Since my auntie Angela has died, the farm now automatically belongs to my mum and I happen to be her legal guardian.

Before Shelley could say anymore, she as rudely interrupted by her crazy uncle who said, “Which Angela are you talking about? Did you kill my oldest wife just to get this farm? What are you trying to do to me? Me and Angela were like twins. These other wives of mine are just bonuses. Angela ran this farm according to my satisfaction. Please tell me she is alive.”

On hearing that the coin was referring to them as just bonuses, some of his wives who were listening to the conversation going on between Shelley and her enemy gathered enough strength to attack him. They were scared of him naturally but because of what he had called them, they all hit him until he bled.

They left him lying on the ground where he had fallen. A few minutes later, his wives summoned him into the house and explained to him what had transpired during his absence. On hearing about his stolen money Mr Sixpence fainted.

“How come he never fainted when we told him that his wife Angela had died? What’s wrong with this beast? Money seems to be more important to him than human lives. When he comes to, lie to him that all his money was stolen because that way he will commit suicide and that’s exactly what we want him to do.” Shelley said as he wiped away the tears on her cheeks as she was still crying for her beloved auntie.

“No, no, no Mr Sixpence is a father. If he didn’t have children, we would definitely allow him to die. All of us his wives we have come to an agreement to just use him as a father figure. We should never have married him in the first place.” Susan explained as she seemed to be on her husband’s side.

The reality was that Susan had a total of sixteen children and she could never imagine life without her husband as she could never be able to rent a house big enough to accommodate her and her offspring.

"Listen you whore, we know you do not love Mr Sixpence. You are taking his side because of your numerous kids. Can't use your brains properly and accept the fact that if Mr Sixpence passes away, which we are all hoping he would, this farm and the money will be shared equally among us all. It's not about who has the most kids with him but it's about who has his blood running through his veins. I made enquiries already the last time I was seeking a divorce after he had given me a good hiding which broke my wrist. My solicitor told me everything. So in case he dies, this farm will be sold and the proceeds shared among us all." Military, one of Mr Sixpence's wives explained.

"All of you are thieves and everything coming out of your mouths is disgusting! Do you hear me? This farm belongs to me and my mother. Nobody and I repeat nobody will take this farm from my mom. We were just keeping you here because of my auntie Angela. We did not feel like ruining her marriage if that's what you call it. I don't even know why my auntie lived with your husband as they never shared the same bedroom. Mr Sixpence only shared the bed with Angela three times in all their married life. She was more of a manager and I wouldn't even put it that way because she was never paid and she spent the last days of her life here on planet earth pick pocket the rubbish bins. Sorry to use that word wrongly. But how would you feel if you saw your own aunt roaming around the city collect rotten food from the bins?" Shelley took a deep breath and went on to say, "This farm will belong to me legally in a few weeks' time and you better take this opportunity to find alternate accommodation."

It seemed Shelley's words had hit home because no one uttered a word after that. They all disappeared and left Shelley guarding her uncle's body. Shelley was eagerly waiting to pass on the message to him. Shelley had a tendency of pouring paraffin onto fire. She had so much wrath in her which many assumed had been caused by her carrying all that burden of caring for a blind mother and at the same time worrying about her aunt who was being abused by Mr Sixpence and it seemed she had no control over it. Shelley wanted to make sure that she retrieved the farm from the coin. As Mr Sixpence was taking long to come to, Shelley fetched cold water and poured a whole gallon on her uncle.

"I said this farm is now legally mine you good for nothing human being. How do you sleep at night knowing that more than a hundred people are grieving over your ill behaviour?" asked Shelley

“Shelly, you will soon see your aunt if you keep harassing me. I have never directly killed anybody except of course, Bertha my other dead wife. Where money is concerned I will definitely kill you. This farm belongs to me and my big family and I will not let a thief like you take it from me. You must never forget that I have maintained this farm using my money and energy and also befo……” Shelley interrupted him before he could finish his speech.

“My mother and I only allowed you to stay here because of my aunt but now that she is gone, I suggest you leave. For the records, we asked you to leave so many times but each time we did, you hit my aunt and threatened her so you could stay on this farm. I gave my solicitor all the paperwork concerning your illegal stay on my farm from the time you moved here including all that transpired during your stay here so that you could not deny. All your replies are with the solicitor and I hid the copies in case the originals get lost. When I deal with a crazy person like you I always find it handy to take extra precautions. Understood!” said Shelley in a very loud voice.

Without saying another word, Mr Sixpence walked into the house where he demanded that four of his wives attend to his small wounds.

CHAPTER FOURTEEN

Mr Sixpence's wives kept a distance as they were scared of revealing the truth about his stolen money.

"Shelley please tell me when my wife Angela will be buried in order for me to make funeral arrangements. Make sure you send messages to the rich only as I don't want those poor rats to come into my yard and waste all my food and toilet paper" said the coin. It seemed as though each time Mr Sixpence opened his mouth lots of idiots popped out.

"What's with you and toilet paper? The main thing is to make the best of this funeral for the sake of you, your neighbours and us, your own family" Ju, one of his wives asked as she was already fed up with her husband and she also went on to say, "Within one hour of your coming you have stressed us all."

"Angela will be buried in two days' time at the city cemetery and we have already bought her coffin" Shelley replied.

"And may I know where you got the money from?" asked the coin.

"We used some of your money from your safe. I hate to tell you this but some of your sons stole your money and left the farm. You knew how much there was and we would appreciate it if you went into your bedroom and count all your money" Ju said and ran outside as she knew her husband would get very angry and maybe take it out on her as he jolly well did each time something went wrong money wise.

"Who knows where these thieves went because I am going to get in my car and follow them. I will make sure they give me all my money back. I will not rest until I have caught them. I am well prepared to go back to prison for my money. No one and I mean no one steals from me and gets away with it. Hear me all!" Mr Sixpence exclaimed as he put his jacket on.

"Sixpence, if you are insane, tell us so we can take you to the insanity institution. How dare you plan a journey in a time like this! Angela is dead and hasn't been buried. Angela is the very reason you are living on this farm. Wait until after her funeral and you can go wherever you want to go. In actual fact, your presence here scares us. You are allowed to disappear forever because we do not care" Ju seemed like she was in a very bad mood and was enjoying tormenting her husband with words.

“By the way the police already know and are looking for your bad mannered children. Give children what they need and they will not be tempted so much to steal. It is your fault, Bertha is dead and it also your fault your sons have turned into ruthless criminals. How can a normal child take a gun and shoot an entire family for the sake of two horses?” Shelley said to her uncle.

“You are going to stay for the funeral and after you have laid my aunt to rest you are very free to go otherwise I will take out my anger of not getting married to you. I d o not have a life, but all I live for is to work and look after my blind mother twenty four hours and seven days a week. You open your mouth one more time and I will use the same gun used by Twoboy to kill you myself, okay” Shelley said and she started crying bitterly.

“Okay, okay, I hear you. I will stay for the funeral. I just have one or two more things I need clarification on. Pardon me and please do not shout at me because I feel like I am back in prison again where there are no polite people and I mean both the staff and the prisoners. Did you say Twoboy and my other sons stole my money and killed my wife Angela for it?” asked the coin while trying to stay calm because he hated it when people shouted at him but enjoyed screaming at others.

“Not only did they pour boiling water on Angela but they killed the entire family next door. All the Ursules are dead except for the mother. Rumour says that if they fail to catch your sons, you, being their father has to pay compensation money for what your sons did” Ju explained as she was doing her best to annoy her husband but soon began to feel sorry for him as the idea of having a husband who had no money nor a farm scared her. On the other hand Shelley was threatening to take the farm away from him and the police were also going to make him pay for the sins his sons had committed.

On hearing this, Mr Sixpence fainted again and an ambulance was called to take him to the city hospital where he stayed for two days. Angela was buried in his absence. There were more than a thousand people who attended Angela’s funeral. Although he had never loved anybody, Mr Sixpence seemed to have been affected badly by Angela’s death or was it because of the farm?

CHAPTER FIFTEEN

The second night before he was officially discharged from hospital, Mr Sixpence had a visitor who was none other than his rude wife Ju. Mr Sixpence had spent the past twenty four hours trying to figure out a way to stop the police getting a glimpse of his money. The idea of them thinking about his money made Mr Sixpence very sick, how about them actually taking his cash from him.

"Ju you always surprise me. You are the last person I expect to get a visit from because all you do is go anti me. You never stop shouting at me and you are always disrespectful of anything I do and may you please tell me the purpose of your visit?" asked Mr Sixpence.

"I didn't sleep at all last night worrying about our future since Shelley and the police are planning to reap you off everything you own and you dare ask me why I am visiting you. When you made married me, you told me you owned the farm and that you were a millionare and that's the reason I actually agreed to marry you. Sixpence honey pie, to tell you the honest truth, I would never have agreed to marry you if it wasn't for the farm because you are never happy; like your other wives, I share the bed with you twice a year and I pay my way in our lives by making money to buy my own food. Pray tell me you will do something to stop the cops taking money from you" Ju replied and she started shedding tears.

"Hey you, stop crying and answer this one question which has been puzzling me. Did the cops actually take finger prints on the crime scene where my boys shot the Ursules?" asked Mr Sixpence.

"What's that got to do with anything? I asked you to tell me my fate and instead of giving me a straight forward answer , you start asking me silly questions about fingerprints. Do I look like a cop to you now? From what I heard, while the police were questioning us concerning Angela's death, the police did not take fingerprints as they were asked to leave the crime scene as they had to attend to a break- in at the big five star hotel - you know the one I am talking about right?. It's that big hotel next to Rocki, the furniture shop" Ju replied but was still feeling a bit confused as to why her husband was so concerned about fingerprints.

"Quickly, pass me my clothes which are in that wardrobe behind you and check out for the nurse while I remove these hospital clothes. Don't say a word. I will explain everything on our way home" said Mr Sixpence.

Both husband and wife used the fire exit to leave the hospital as the coin had discharged himself. On their way back home Mr Sixpence explained that he was going to set fire to the house next door to his farm where Twoboy, his son had shot all the family members.

“Do you realise what you have just done? You invited the police into your life again. I am beginning to think you are doing this deliberately so you can go back to prison where you get everything for free. Am I wrong n thinking that?” asked one of his numerous wives.

“It’s exactly the opposite of what you are thinking. Actually, I am driving the police away from my life permanently. Ask me why? After erasing all fingerprints from the crime scene, there is no way the police can connect me and my family to the deaths of the Ursule family. I always use my loaf wisely. Ask me any questions on saving money and I will gladly tell you. The cops will be arriving next door soon and everyone here you saw nothing okay” said Mr Sixpence as he was still in shock after realising what he had done. Mr Sixpence was under the impression that Mrs Ursules had been burnt to death.

The local police arrived and started doing their job. One of the police opened the garage door and saw Mrs Ursules groaning in pain. She could not talk as she was bleeding heavily from her mouth and it seemed she had lost most of her teeth. Mrs Ursules was pointing her finger at the garage door. The policeman walked to where Mrs Ursules was pointing and saw the word ‘coin’. Before the policeman could get any further questions from her, she fell into a coma.

An ambulance was called and Mrs Ursules body was carried to the nearest hospital. After checking on all their needed to check on, the policemen proceeded on around the village asking questions. One close friend of the Ursules family whom had been hurt by the death of his friend told them that ‘coin’ was a nickname for Mr Sixpence.

Mr Sixpence was arrested immediately. During the court trial, the jury hardly found anything to connect him to the crime scene so he was just given a four months sentence. Mr Sixpence’s jail sentence was given on the understanding that there was no way Mrs Ursules could have written Mr Sixpence’s nickname while she was in pain. It had to be a name of someone she had seen just before her farm was set on fire.

CHAPTER SIXTEEN

Four months soon elapsed and Mr Sixpence was released from Prison. He went back to his farm a different man. He was so determined to get every penny from anyone who had stolen his money. Mr Sixpence new dictionary lacked the words *defeat and failure.*

The same he arrived back at his house he summoned all his family and had a big meeting which took forever.

During the meeting it was agreed that Tsano, one of his many sons get a job as a Director in the Village Bank where Mr Sixpence's friend worked as a Managing Director.

Mr Sixpence chose five of his boys to work in the same bank with their brother Tsano. The five sons were given jobs in the security department and monitoring computers. People believed the coin's family used voodoo to get jobs not realising that Mr Sixpence bribed his friends to give his family jobs. Mr Sixpence was a member of the mafias who made it a point to protect their own.

Tsano was trusted with all the keys and combination to the bank safe. Like their mothers, the Sixpence boys were hard workers and it left Mr Braeside no choice but to like them and trust them with all combination and password details. In other words the security system was controlled by the Sixpence boys.

Mr Sixpence made it his job to get rich customers for the bank where his sons worked. Almost all the farmers took their business to the Village bank. Mr Sixpence took the liberty of surfing the world wide web seeking to rich customers abroad to have shares in the Village bank.

The Sixpence boys' target was more than two million pounds. It took less than nine months for the bank to have the kind of money they were expecting to steal.

On October 24, 2084, the worst robbery took place at the Village bank, as the newspapers later explained. While Tsano was preparing to close business for the day, a group of youths entered his bank, gave Tsano a terrible hiding including the security officers who were none else than Tsano's brothers. The robbers took the safe keys from them and got away with the money. According to plan, the police were called four hours later after making sure that the robbers were way away from the crime scene.

Questions were still being raised by the public as to how the alarm system had not gone off. It was assumed by many that Tsano's brothers who worked as computer operators had fiddled with the alarm systems of the entire building. The robbers had got away with a total amount of two million five hundred thousand pounds and ninety four pennies.

Mr Sixpence had regained all his money but this time with plenty of interest. As if that was not enough, Mr Sixpence called for another meeting and told his family that they had to find his missing sons and retrieve all the money they had stolen from his safe.

"In my entire life I have never come across anyone as ridiculous and impossible as you. Are you still not happy with all that money your wizards stole from the Village bank? The whole neighbourhood is still talking about it you now. The name coin is not a good fitting nickname for you. From today on we will call you Beelzebub. I think and I am beginning to believe that when Lucifer and two thirds of the heavenly angels were thrown out of heaven, they all entered into your body. I have tried to figure out who you are and I have failed. You want money but you do not want to use it. Money is meant to look after you and not you looking after it. You are a millionaire and we, your family enjoy just one meal a day. What are you breathing oxygen for? On Sunday you and your family will take a trip to the local church and have the Reverend lay hands on you" Ju said as she was the only one who had guts to attack him.

"No one will take me to that church of yours. All they want is to take money from people and…" before he could finish saying whatever he wanted to say Ju interrupted and said, "Listen to the pot calling the kettle black. What did you just say? You don't want people to take money from other people. I can't believe you actually said that. Who in this entire world takes money from people besides you Demon? We all work for you. You make it your business to take our every penny. You are a moving grave because no thinking person would talk like that. I hate you Demon" Ju carried on shouting at her husband.

As he was scared of Ju shouting at him, Mr Sixpence visited the local Pastor of the Pentecostal church and begged him to hold church meeting in his own house. The thought of boarding a bus with his big family and paying transport expenses scared him. The reverend came of course and was glad to preach a sermon at the Sixpence farm.

The first Sunday after preaching, Ju made the Reverend a cup of tea and served it with cream cracker biscuits. As there were some family members who had repented according to the Bible Chapter Acts 2 verse 38, Ju thought of making tea for everyone. Her main aim was to cover her husband's evil ways by making the Reverend believe that Mr Sixpence was a good husband. Ju's friend had told her that Preachers are very powerful instruments used by the government and if they find any abused wives or children, they would make a note of it and inform the social services who would then take further action by either taking all the children away from their parents and maybe arrest the parents. Since the toilets were smelly and not cared for, she definitely knew that the farm would be closed down. That scared Ju so much such that she promised herself she was going to create an impression of a happy family.

After the reverend was gone, Shelley walked into the kitchen to find her uncle Mr Sixpence holding a calculator as he was counting how many tea bags had been used by the Reverend and his own family.

"What are you doing?" asked Shelley.

"I am counting the number of tea bags used by my family. I told you all that we only have tea once a month. Ju never ever listens to me. She invited the Reverend and on top of that used my milk, my tea bags and my water. I told you all that my visitors should bring their own food and toilet paper and if they need to have tea, like those greedy priests, who are not man enough to drink beer but drink tea instead, they should bring their own milk and cups. No more church meetings okay. I can't afford. Surely, he is a man of God. He has the ability to know what I think doesn't he? He should very well know that I don't want people using my things!" Mr Sixpence said that and banged the kitchen table with his bare fist.

Shelley walked out without saying anymore and she went in the back garden to sit with her mum. At this point in time, she really envied her mom's blindness. She was lucky to be blind because if she wasn't, she would be shocked to see Mr Sixpence counting tea bags.

CHAPTER SEVENTEEN

Since he was making a big deal about his money being spent by church people but at the same time forgetting that they would bring joy, peace and happiness to his family, Shelley decided to help aunt's children by starting a business of their own where they would not need to use the coin's money. After spending some time at the farm with the mad man and realising how ridiculous he was Shelley suddenly realised why her aunt sacrificed her happiness for her husband's wives and children. Angela was not stupid after all but instead she lived on the farm to help the family. Mr Sixpence's family were being controlled, abused, starved and not cared for. Shelley anger was slowly turning to sympathy.

Shelley now had two thoughts running through her mind – whether to be authorised by the law to keep the farm under her own name and live on it but still being controlled by Mr Sixpence or to get rid of Mr Sixpence only. The only way to get rid of the coin was by selling the farm to a total stranger altogether. Shelley knew that as long as his wives and children were on the farm, Mr Sixpence would use them as an excuse to stay on the farm and keep an eye on his family. As she waited for her appointment with her solicitor, Shelley thought of opening a graveyard business for the Sixpence family.

It seemed Shelley had turned into a crook herself. The Sixpence family business involved burying the dead day time and same day in the evening, steal the coffins and resell them to new dead people's relatives.

CHAPTER SEVENTEEN

While Shelley was busy making money for her aunt Angela's children, Mr Sixpence was busy thinking of other ways to make money for himself. The thought of attacking Shelley scared him because he knew that crossing Shelley's path meant death or torture. He decided not to attack Shelley's business but to wait awhile until later. Actually, he was planning to marry her because he knew that by marrying Shelley, he would still own the farm and take over the business Shelley and his family were running.

After many sleepless nights, Mr Sixpence was pleased to come out with a plan which he knew would get rid of most of his children since he did not feel like maintaining.

As usual a meeting was called and everyone went to sit outside while enjoying the sun.

"You are not going to make us pay for the sunshine, dad are you?" asked Ju, his naughty wife.

"If it wasn't for the stupid government laws that make a husband maintain a wife after divorce, I would have got rid of you a long time ago. Because it's cheaper for me to keep you on this farm, I shall not divorce you but will stay with you until your death. Also if I divorced you, I will not be able to get insurance money on your life policy. Actually I gain more by you living on my farm and buying your own food. Curse me as much as you want, but I will never divorce you" said the horrible Mr Sixpence.

"I don't remember me having an insurance policy. You live in a dream world you wizard!" replied Ju.

"Oh Ju, your ignorance makes me want to vomit sometimes. I made sure all of you my wives have life policies. I am not responsible for you not being able to read and write. Remember those forms, I made you sign thinking it was my will? They were life policy forms. There is nothing any of you can do about it. According to the law, your signatures on those forms are legitimate. That cheque brought to me this morning was from the Insurance guys and it's money from Angela's life policy" said Mr Sixpence feeling very proud of himself.

Shelley and Ju and the other wives stood up and all at once said, "We are going to phone the police".

"I would not do that if I were any of you. You want to know why, because Angela signed me as a beneficiary. Actually we were witnessed by a solicitor. You can never prove that I tricked her because the solicitor asked her to raise her hand if she agreed and she did. The only crime I commited was educating her on our way by lying to her that it was my will and if she opened her mouth, the solicitor will end up asking her if I had other wives. All she had to do was to say yes to anything the solicitors asked her" Mr Sixpence said and the angry wives sat down feeling very defeated.

"Just tell us how you made the rest of us sign" asked Ju.

"Remember that time I told you my mother had cancer and I was asking you to sign your names individually so in case I died the money would go to you. Those forms were actually life policy documents. Anyway why would you worry? You will be dead and gone and I just enjoy your money. It's not as though you worked for the money. That kind of money is just like a bonus. Try not to waste any more of my time as I have better things to do" Mr Sixpence carried on tormenting hi wives and it seemed as though he was enjoying it.

Shelley could do nothing but just weep. Discovering live Mr Sixpence was making her more and more sympathetic of the Sixpence wives and children. Shelley was just waiting for her appointment with the solicitor as the secretary told her that he had gone on a cruise. Shelley's solicitor was due back from his holiday in a couple of days and that eased her blood pressure.

Everyone sat quietly as they listened to the 'coin' dictating what he wanted his family do.

The plan was that his handsome sons fall in love with married rich wives. After a few dates with them, they would ensure the husband catch them red handed. A divorce would soon be certain. After the divorce, the rich men's ex-wives would be married to Mr Sixpence's sons. On the other hand, the divorced husbands would be married to the Sixpence daughters.

On hearing the evil plans, his entire family wept bitterly. It was like they were mourning a dead close relative.

The dating business started and within a few months many married rich couples were divorced.

Most of his married children who had been part of the dating game took this opportunity to leave the country were they were living and moved to other countries where their father found it hard or impossible to visit them. On one side they were happy he had opened doors for them to enjoy luxurious living but on the other hand they hated him for who he was. They wished they had married under normal circumstances. Each time they looked at their partners they felt guilty because they had got them to marry them in very deceitful ways. The Sixpence daughters like any other females quickly adjusted to enjoying married life but the boys found it hard but could not divorce because divorcing their partners meant them going back to their father and suffer under his laws.

Years and years later, the children born to the dating game children soon grew older and most attended Universities for the simple reason that their parents could afford and also they had no rush to get jobs as they had all the money they needed to last them a life time.

It so happened that two of the Sixpence grandchildren from the union of the dating game children attended the same University. Their names were Jill and John. They met and fell head over heels in love with each other. A month into their relationship, Jill got pregnant. As they each proclaimed to be religious people they decided to wed before Jill's tummy got big.

Messages were sent to the entire Sixpence family home and abroad.

The wedding day was set giving enough time for the relatives to arrive and witness the marriage of Jill and John. A big hall was hired and even the Queen was invited.

Jill's parents and John's parents were given adjacent rooms in the hotel that had been booked for close family members. On the night of the wedding everyone arrived.

"Hi Tracy. What are you doing here? These rooms are reserved for the parents of the bride and groom. Jill is my daughter and that room you are opening has been reserved for John's parents" asked Jill's dad who was none other than Mr Sixpence's son.

"It so happens that John is my son. Wait a minute. Did you say that you are Jill's dad? I don't believe this. You mean John and Jill are actually first cousins. Just go out there and call off the wedding" said Jill's mother.

“I could but I just discovered that Jill is pregnant. Her doctor is a friend of ours” said John’s father.

Since the bride and bride groom parents were both Sixpences by blood or by law via marriage, they decided to seek their father’s advice since he was very good at solving impossible problems.

“Wait after the wedding and we will take some action then. Our visitors have brought wedding gifts and my pigeon instinct tells me some will be donating cash instead of gifts. It is against my rules to let easy money go by. All you have to do is stay in your rooms and Jill and john will never know that there are related” said Mr Sixpence.

“But how come the bride and groom never realised they were related? They both use the name Sixpence right?” asked John’s wife.

“Dad, I hate to say this but because of the dating game which in actual fact made us marry our partners, we decided to change our last names because most people were talking about it. Most of us your children changed our names and because friends still recognised us, we eventually agreed we would be safe moving to other countries were nobody knew us” replied Jill’s mother.

“It’s too late to stop the wedding now. We have to recover all the money we used to hire the hall and hotel accommodation and you two couples stay in your rooms. I will give the bride away myself” said Mr Sixpence.

“You will never change will you? It’s all about money to you, isn’t it? Nothing else matters to you except money” replied his daughter.

It so happened that Jill had been listening to every word being said between her parents, John’s parents and her grandfather. Without uttering a word, she went in her hotel room, packed her bags and disappeared and no one ever saw her again. The wedding could not go on without the bride so everyone was asked to go back to their homes.

“That little witch made me lose a lot of money. If I find her, I will sue her and demand all the money which the wedding guests were supposed to donated” Mr Sixpence said. Mr Sixpence went to the hotel reception and made an announcement requiring the wedding guests to leave their gifts behind.

Ju persuaded Mr Sixpence' rich sons to buy their father some whisky and at the same time sit with him until he was drunk because that way everyone would feel safe without him misbehaving and saying all the wrong things.

CHAPTER EIGHTEEN

Months later, the run away bride gave birth to a baby boy and advertised to her doctor that she wanted her son adopted by a good family who could take care of it. The thought of raising that child gave her the chills because each time she looked at him, she was reminded of her grandfather's evilness. Unfortunately enough for her, the doctor was none other than a mafia member where Mr Sixpence was also a mafia.

The runaway bride had made the mistake of explaining to the doctor why she needed to have her son adopted.

Mr Sixpence asked a friend to take him to the maternity hospital where mother and child were being kept because the baby had been delivered by caesarean methods.

"We the Sixpences care for our own and this what you are trying to do is not allowed. I will not allow you to sell my grandson. You stay in hospital and I will take my grandson with me to be raised by my wives, agreed!" said Mr Sixpence to Jill, his granddaughter who was a product of the dating games.

Mr Sixpence asked his friend to pass through the social services offices.

"Why on earth should we pass through the city instead of just driving straight home with the poor baby. He must be very hungry by now or have you forgotten that you stole him from his mother with your mouth. I like the way you steal. You actually cause your victims to give you money or whatever you want from them" said Mr Sixpence's friend.

"Listen the whole aim of adopting my own grand son was to have him registered as mine and he will be paid benefit money – you know what I am talking about. Did you not know that our stupid government actually pay us for sleeping with our wives and having babies? I keep all my children and grandchildren so I can make money from them via social services" replied Mr Sixpence.

They passed through the social services offices and the new baby was registered as Mr Sixpence's dependent and a cheque for one hundred and twenty pounds was given to him. Mr Sixpences was also reminded that he had to expect cheques from the social services weekly for his grandson for the next sixteen years.

"In other words, you did not want your grandson but you actually wanted him for the money you can steal from the government. How low can a human being sink?" said Mr Sixpence's concerned friend.

“It’s not my fault that the government officials are thick. Can you explain this to me – I sleep with my own wives and enjoy myself. The government who were never a part of the sex game thank me by paying me for the pleasures I had with my own wives. Did you see or hear what the receptionist said? She actually demanded that I wait for the cheque and cash it today. I am their best customer because I have had all my 166 (one hundred and sixty six children raised by the stupid social services. If its handed to me freely on a plate, I take it. That’s my motto” said Mr Sixpence as he smoked his tobacco pipe.

“Do you love anybody and by loving I mean having feelings for human beings or it’s just having people in your life which you need to use? I feel sorry for your family and like Shelley said, I quote, ‘My aunt Angela wanted to leave you so many times but because she felt sorry for your wives and children she decided to carry on living with you just so she could be there for them. You are a moving grave. That’s right because it’s actually the dead who cannot feel anything for anybody” said his friend and he decided to stay silent for the rest of their journey back home.

When Mr Sixpence got home, he summoned Ju and asked her to raise the new baby boy as her own. That way Mr Sixpence felt it wise to keep Ju occupied twenty four hours a day and that meant no mouthing from her. Mr Sixpence was allergic to criticism.

Mr Sixpence carried on with his life as normal which involved visiting the social welfare every Monday collecting cheques for his family. Neighbours wondered why he was never caught because to get government help, one had to be penniless.

Mr Sixpence’s reply was, “My money stays in my safe an when the welfare people ask me for a bank statement, I show them one which has a bank balance of £0.06. My bank account balance stays at six pence. If they don’t pay me, I will definitely sue them.”

Mr Sixpence’s family, under the command of Shelley thought it best to ignore him. Shelley made it a point to prepare three meals a day. Shelley built a small kitchen just outside her offices in the cemetery where she was burying the dead and reselling the coffins.

As business was blossoming, Shelley built a crematorium where she burnt the dead bodies but made sure the gold teeth of the riches were kept for her other second hand shop in the city. Shelley’s shop sold everything from gold teeth to stolen goods.

CHAPTER NINETEEN

The day arrived for Shelley and her blind mother to visit their solicitor for the purposes of reclaiming their farm and putting Shelly's name on the farm's title deeds.

The Silicitor's secretary telephoned the farm to remind Shelley that her appointment was due the very next day. Unfortunately, it so happened that when the soliitor's secretary phoned, Shelley was away and Mr Sixpence answered the phone.

"Hello, who is this?" asked Mr Sixpence.

"It's the Smart solicitors and can I have a word with Shelley?" came the reply from the other end of the line.

"Shelley is away at the moment but can I take a message? I am her work mate. Shelley invited me here to help with her new business" replied the coin.

"Please tell Shelley that she must not forget her appointment with Mr Smart her solicitor. Please do me this one favour – don't tell her uncle about it otherwise he will do everything in his power to stop her from attending the meeting. Much obliged" pleaded the solicitor's secretary.

"Just in time. That was close" said Mr Sixpence as he spoke to himself after putting back the receiver.

After scratching his head and coming out with nothing, Mr Sixpence finally came out with a plan which he believed was going to help him save his farm. Mr Sixpence decided it was best that he marry Shelley and give her many babies. By so doing he had nothing to lose. In fact, that plan made him realise how he was going to gain from his marriage to Shelley – a hard working wife who made money for herself and other people's children and on top of that children who would be paid wages they never worked for. Moreover, the government would pay Shelley's biological children money every week and for the next eighteen years.

"Why not enjoy my lo9ve life and be paid for it by my wives and their children who work hard to feed themselves and also the stupid government which pay them monies for breathing oxygen from the moment they are born" the coin smiled to himself as he said that.

Mr Sixpence visited the cemetery and picked up some flowers from one of the graves and took them to Shelley.

"What are these flowers for?" asked Shelley who was busy preparing dinner for her big family.

"I bought them for you. Aren't they nice? I was just missing you and thinking of what a beautiful body you have" replied Mr Sixpence.

"Don't even think it. You are lying to me. You took these flowers from Mr Ink's grave. Do you want to know how I know? Mr Ink's widow was too sick to go to the flower shop and she asked me to buy her those flowers and I am the one who put them on her husband's grave. You thief!" said Shelley.

"Relax, just relax. Like Mrs Ink, I did not have time to go to the city to buy you flowers and I just said to myself, 'the dead man can't smell the flowers and he can't even see them as I believe he is six feet under so let me take the liberty of giving the flowers to my beloved Shelley and make a good use of them because you can smell their scent with your nose. Was I wrong in doing that? Honestly, I did not mean any harm. But may accept my apologies if I offended you. If you give me one minute, I will explain the purpose of my visit. You will definitely like the news" said Mr Sixpence in a romantic voice.

"Stop playing the saint with me okay! Why do you always justify your wrong doings? Everybody else is an idiot except you. You are disgusting. Just ...." Before she could finish whatever she was about to say, Mr Sixpence grabbed her and kissed her.

"What the hell are you doi..." Shelley tried to free herself but the coin was too clever for her because he carried her into the small kitchen and made passionate love to her.

Shelley wished she had been born a man. She hated herself for giving in to Mr Sixpence. Like her departed aunt, Angela, she just gave in easily to the horrible man.

What have I done now? I just hope I am not pregnant. Why on earth did you do that for? I am like a traitor now – joining hands with the enemy. What will your wives and children think if they realise I am now wife number 123? We have teamed up against you. You are unbelievably evil!" said Shelley as she was feeling uncomfortable with the current situation she was in.

"Never mind my wives. They are all psychos and very stupid. If they say the wrong things, I will just ask them to leave and they know they dare not go over the limit with me. Who in this day and age will marry a mother with a bunch of kids?" said Mr Sixpence as he seemed to be feeling proud of himself in what he had just done. Little did Shelley know that her union with the coin was because he wanted to save his farm from the law.

Shelley asked Mr Sixpence what he was going to do with her and her baby in case she was pregnant.

“Shelley oh Shelley ever since I set my eyes on you when I first knew your late aunt Angela, I have been waiting for a moment like this. I could not do it then because you were just a young confused girl. But I told myself that the day that girl turns eighteen I will definitely marry her. The problem I later faced was you shouting at me each time we meant then I realised you did not like me and that really put me off” explained the coin and Shelley seemed to enjoy listening the sweet things coming from the coin.

“What will I tell my solicitor whom I have given a very negative picture of you? When I meet him soon, I will just have to tell him the truth” said Shelley.

“Why do you fear someone whom you pay to do the work for you? Are you like these idiots of citizens who fear government officials who do nothing but take money from them? Tell me something, I have often wondered why citizens world wide fear their leaders? Who is supposed to be in charge? The one who pays the money or the recipient? If I have my servants and pay them for their services, I would never allow them to control me. Am I right? All leaders are supposed to be under your authority and by this I mean they are paid to do what you want and not you to do what they want. They are just ordinary human beings like you and I am quite sure you confuse them by fearing them” as he carried on explaining Shelley was beginning to agree with him. Mr Sixpence was very good at brainwashing but whatever he said always made sense.

“Part of me really wants to strangle you but something else tells me to go ahead with your plan of us getting married. At least I can still carry on caring for your wives and children whom you do not care about. If you are so intelligent, why is it you do not feed your wives and children?” asked Shelley.

“Most of my wives were rough sleepers and some were prostitutes. Believe me Shelley they are now living better lives than they did before I married them. Why do you think they never leave me? I never keep them under lock and key neither do I tie chains around their wrists and ankles. Even you are lucky to have a rich husband like me. My wives complain because I hardly spent time with them. All women like their husband’s attention and that’ the only problem they have. They are away all day long making money for me but ask them why they come back to me? I am a good husband Shelley. You live with me full time and I will prove it to you” replied the coin.

“I am getting more and more confused. Please stop talking now and go back home because I have to finish making dinner for your family or my family as I will now be a part of them legally. I do not know what my mother will think of me but I know that I will have answers to my problems by morning" Shelley said.

-62-

Without wasting any more time, Mr Sixpence spent the night in Shelley's bedroom and not because he wanted to marry her but because he wanted to be the one in charge of her dead corpses' business. By noon the following day, Shelley and every thing about her belonged to Mr Sixpence.

A fortnight later, they were married and then after putting a ring on her finger, Mr Sixpence thought of taking revenge on Shelley's solicitor whom he hated as he was trying to get the farm off him. Mr and Mrs new Sixpence visited the solicitor's office and Mr Sixpence proudly introduced himself as Shelley's husband and asked the solicitor to make a will concerning the farm.

Shelley's solicitor who was well aware of Mr Sixpence's wickedness refused to do the will business with him but referred him elsewhere. Shelley did nothing but look down all the time her husband was talking to the solicitors not because he wanted to but because he was just taking revenge.

"Did you have to do that? Anyway, my solicitor's secretary told me that they left a message for me a few days ago for my appointment with them do you know whom they spoke to?" asked Shelley.

"It's not important now Shelley my favourite wife. We will go back to our farm and enjoy life as usual. Look at you, you have gained a lot of weight since moving to my farm. I told you I am a very good husband. You were very thin when you first came after your aunt passed away but now your legs are like elephant trunks" said the coin feeling very proud of himself and at the same time taking credit for what other people did.

"You are so amazing aren't you? I have gained extra weight because me and your other wives decided we work hard, make lots of money and enjoy three meals a day not just one. One more word from you and I will contact my lawyer for a divorce" at the mention of divorce which meant him losing the farm and maintaining Shelley's child made the coin realise that he had to shut his mouth.

Shelley's sudden outburst scared him so much that he persuaded Shelley to pass by her doctor's surgery for pregnancy test. Mr Sixpence had listened several times to his dead wife each time she told him that Shelley had vowed that if she ever got married she would always love her husband and keep him so her children could enjoy having both father and mother. Shelley's biological father had married a second wife and Shelley had been left to care for a blind mother all by herself and still suffer from living without a dad. Shelley getting pregnant by him meant keeping her for good. According to his wishes, her tests proved positive. Shelley was pregnant. Mr Sixpence grabbed her and kissed her tenderly. All this fake love was done to keep his farm.

-63-

If Shelley had taken a knife and cut Mr Sixpence's chest cavity, she would have been very shocked to see his heart and discover what it was he really wanted from her. Angela, her aunt had always told her this saying 'what the eyes had not seen the heart could not grieve'. Through those wise sayings, Shelley had always tried not to be too inquisitive.

Mr Sixpence was now the new boss of the crematorium business. Mr Sixpence met some of his doctor friends at the local pub and shared ideas about anything in life like the drunkards always did although they never put most of it into practice.

One Friday evening at the pub, Mr Sixpence was shocked to hear that they were doctors who made friends with witch doctors who needed human body parts to enable them run their witch business.

"I run a crematorium business and I can make a business deal with you. Listen this is what we are going to do. Instead of burning the dead body, I will swap the dead body for a wild animal and keep the corpse for you and you give me the money" Mr Sixpence said as he spoke to the witch doctors.

"What if the relatives find out?" asked one of the witch doctors.

"What planet do you come from? These people are illiterate and tell me how in the name of God they will discover that the ashes they have belong to a wild animal?" Mr Sixpence asked.

"Deal. I just wanted to make sure that's all. You don't have to scream at me, you know" said the other witch doctor who lived not far from where the coin lived.

"Mr Sixpence, you do realise that this is a very dangerous business because if caught you will be pulvirised by not only the relatives of the dead but also the law and no one in this world will ever trust you. You will be lucky to come out of prison" said Shorty one of the doctors.

"What are you talking about? I heard one cannot be arrested for harming a dead body. That person is rotting anyway so what difference will it make? Don't tell me you believe in what these government people say. Aren't they the ones going around the world killing innocent souls in the name of a war? Please explain something to me. When two countries offend each other by way of leaders, who suffers? It's the innocent citizens who never know or see their leader but they will be the ones suffering and dying for what their leaders say to their enemies. My motto remains and I have taught my many wives and children that I do not vote for any one politically. Have you ever heard of a President's son going to fight and be put on the front line?

-64-

The day I hear that my President is wearing camouflage and holding a gun fighting the enemy, I will definitely join them but before then I don't like them and I never trust them and so does my family who live under my roof. Why have you all suddenly gone quiet? I thought you said I have done a very bad thing by selling someone who is already dead. My victims are dead people whereas the political leaders' victims are living people. These soldiers have wife and young kids. Who will compensate for the widows of the dead soldiers whose children have to suffer without a father and live under the rule of a step father? Money cannot bring back a loved one. Whatever you say, I feel justified for my actions and I never feel guilty about it. That's why I steal from them money which they keep and which they never worked for. I will give you homework for the night and it goes like this; tell me any leader in this entire world who does voluntary work or any leader who is not paid by innocent citizens? We work day and night making money while they sit in their offices making our lives a misery by passing laws which make it hard for us to survive on planet earth! If you don't want business with me, I will find other sensible people who have the same beliefs as me" said Mr Sixpence as he sipped a glass of Fanta bought for him by his friend.

"You did not have to give us a long lecture! Gees, you are so full of vernom. I am now starting to understand you and to like you a little but keep your opinions to yourself because in this world the politicians are deadly and don't you ever forget that" said Mr Shorty.

"It's people like you who promote corruption and confuse your leaders. Instead of them fearing you, you confuse them by placing a red carpet each time they visit you at their silly rallies. All your leaders are not Samson alright? What I mean is how can thirty three million normal people live under fear of a couple of government staff? Common sense tells me that thirty three million individuals are well able to attack and destroy less than hundred people who rule you. Why is everyone so brainless? I was reading the newspaper yesterday where the people of Plep, that country north of ours were suffering under the rule of their ninety four year old Prime Minister for over forty years now. After reading that article about the Plep people I burnt my newspaper because I failed to understand why the entire nation were not fighting physically and getting rid of a useless leader who was making their lives a misery for more than two decades. If you ever want my friendship don't talk politic to me" as he said this, Mr Sixpence called it a day and went home.

The following day just before noon Mr Sixpence was surprised to see his doctor friends come to visit him.

"After you left last night we thought about all you said and we realised that you were right. It all makes sense but people are not united enough to fight the leaders. Anyway we won't go into that as we want to check if it's still alright with you to carry on with our business plans. You know the one we mean – selling body parts?" asked Mr Shorty.

"I never say no to money. My name says it all – Sixpence – coin – money. We will not do any signing in case we are caught as that will be very damaging evidence. Okay mates, do visit me tonight as they are burying those three soldiers who were killed during the war in Retu. Retu right? I am not quite sure about the name but it's that country north of ours. I have told my workers to reserve the bodies for you. I think it's better you leave now because I have this one crazy wife of mine who makes it her business to know what I am doing and then shouts at me in public. You can honestly have her if you want. If it wasn't for my grandson which she is raising, I would definitely hire the mafia to get rid of her and then claim insurance money on her life policy. She makes my life a misery. Enough for now, by the way do not forget that we have a meeting tonight guys" said the coin.

As agreed the coin left half an hour early for the graveyard where he and his friends had planned to steal the bodies of the three soldiers killed in war.

"Why are you giggling to yourselves? Do I smell or not because if I smell it's only because of the pipe as my twins who work in the hotel brought them for me. Can we please share the joke as I like that joke the same as the next ugly person" said Mr Sixpence.

"No, you are very mistaken. Actually we spent all afternoon discussing what you said last night about thirty three million people failing to kill just one hundred people who make their lives a living hell. The funniest bit was the one where you said that we actually pay them to ruin our lives" replied Mr Shorty.

"You think that's funny, wait till you hear this one which one of my stupid son said in a class full of his mates. The teacher asked him to name three types of animals which live in the river and he said, '1. crocodile, 2. fish' and the teacher said, I asked for three' then he said number 3 is another crocodile' " said Mr Sixpence and he went on to say, "I don't think that stupid boy is my son because all my children are intelligent like me. The midwives at the clinic he was born must have swapped him and I got the stupid one and my own intelligent son is somewhere out there being raised by some stupid parents. It's just like Twoboy and Frank, my two boys. How could they kill my oldest wife, Angela for just nine hundred pounds? Can you believe that kind of stupidity? For a million pounds yes but just nine hundred pounds and if caught they serve life in prison?"

"Your vocabulary is terrible, my friend. Do you have to use the word 'stupid' all the time? You hate it when Ju, your wife screams at you and I am sure people don't like it when you call them stupid" replied one of his criminal friends.

"Call me names if you want but I know that I never call people names when they haven't done anything wrong. Ju, my wife calls me names all the time. I promised myself that if I see my stupid sons, I will kill them myself with my bare hands" replied the coin.

-66-

"I don't even know why we are even bothering arguing with you. You have to win all the arguments, don't you? Anyway, the other guys have finished digging the three graves and I think we will take over from them and put the corpses in the boots of our cars. Next time, please don't hire other people to help with digging because you never know whom they will tell" one of the friends said as he helped with the dead bodies. Mr Sixpence kept the coffins and said farewell to his partners in crime.

As he got home, Mr Sixpence suddenly realised that he had not been paid for the dead bodies. He quickly got on the phone and rang Mr Shorty.

"What game are you playing? You have evidence on you that you stole dead bodies. I will call the cops and tell them that you stole the bodies and when I caught you red handed, you left the coffins and fled with the dead bodies. You are the doctors and I am not" said the furious coin.

"What the hell are you talking about?" asked Mr Shorty.

"Don't talk to me like I was born yesterday and never forget this one thing, I am a mafia gangster" replied the coin.

"I said what exactly are you talking about?" Mr Shorty kept asking as he did not know what his friend wanted from him.

"Money! I said I want my payment for the three dead soldiers you stole from my graveyard and I am coming right now to fetch it. I will also need a further four pounds for my fuel which I am going to waste for the journey to your house. Understood!" Mr Sixpence said and immediately left for Shorty's house.

Shorty was already waiting for the coin outside his house. Mr Shorty knew that when the coin was angry, he never minced his words and he also registered his anger by screaming and that he never cared whether he was in public or not.

Within minutes the coin arrived and Mr Shorty handed him the cheque.

"I just feel sorry for your wives and kids. I don't know how they manage to live with a thing like you because you are so impossible. One minute you are laughing and the very next minute you are angry and for no apparent reason. Me and the guys knew the banks were closed and were going to cash that cheque tomorrow and give you cash. We would never deliberately annoy you. Do you still want to carry on as partners or we end it right now? You really scared me. It's a good job my wife and kids were asleep otherwise what was I going to tell them? My wife is a strong Christian and I don't want to bother her with my sins.

She believes I am a good husband and it stays like that. I am different from you because you let your wives know your bad parts and do you want to know the truth? Your wives stopped loving and trusting you a long time ago. Women only want to hear the good side about anything. I am a deacon in the Church my wife and kids attend and as long as she is happy with me, it stays that way. Tell me, why should I let her know that I steal dead bodies and I drink dead people's blood? It will kill her because to her I am her hero and even after I die she will have sweet memories of me. I know I am headed for hell but she does not have to suffer for my sins. Take my advice and see how your wives can turn into queens who will make you so happy and erase the sadness in you" Mr Shorty said and went back into his house.

Mr Shorty's long lecture had taken effect on Mr Sixpence as he spent the next couple of days treating his wives like queens.

CHAPTER TWENTY

Mr Sixpence lacked tactics most times and would end up exaggerating whatever game he was playing. Mr Shorty's advice was working well to his favour except for one thing and that was showing more love to Shelley. His other wives couldn't take it. Mr Sixpence was now spending more time at the graveyard with Shelley and when Shelley was nine months pregnant, Mr Sixpence gave her the keys to his safe and asked her to keep an eye on his money and the toilet rolls.

"What's it with you and toilet rolls? Why do toilet rolls mean so much to you?" asked Shelley.

"The thing is – toilet rolls enable me to realise how much food my family is spending. The more toilet rolls they use the more I discover that they are having three meals a day. The other thing is when anyone knows they are no toilet rolls in the toilet, they won't eat much because they will be rest assured that it won't be wise to use a toilet and not have something to clean your bum with" said Mr Sixpence.

"All I can say is you are amazing" replied Shelley.

Shelley was ordered to manage the farm the same way her auntie Angela hade been doing.

One day while on her rounds checking stock of the cash, Shelley noticed a big brown envelope hidden in the safe. Being the nosy person she was, Shelley opened the envelope and looked at the contents. Shelley was so shocked and hardly believed her eyes when she read the contents and realised that the farm had been sold to Funny, Mr Sixpence's prodigal son.

"How dare he trick me like this?" said Shelley to herself and she sat on the bed and wept bitterly. Like all abused women or in this case a used woman as she was not paid for her services, Shelley made a plan and that plan was to kill Mr Sixpence. Shelley was gong to poison Mr Sixpence's food. After killing Mr Sixpence, Shelley' next plan was to get rid of Funny and she shelved that idea until further notice. Shelley suddenly realised that Mr Sixpence was right when he had always said that Shelley, her blind mother and her auntie Angela were nothing but stupid people who allowed people to use them and not only them but also their monies including anything they owned. Shelley also realised that she was being taken for a ride and that ride had a dead end to it.

Even in his early nineties, Mr Sixpence kept impregnating young girls and asking them to move in with him and share his farm.

-69-

All Mr Sixpence wanted was more young children to earn government money. Mr Sixpence always panicked when any of his children turned eighteen because it meant the government not paying them.

One Sunday morning, while making preparations to go for mass at the Roman Catholic church in their neighbourhood, Shelley was heard by one of Mr Sixpence's wives, plotting to get rid of him by poisoning his food with rat poison.

The wives quickly ran and informed their husband of Mr Sixpence's favourite wife's deadly idea. Mr Sixpence was always a step in front of his enemies. After realising what had triggered Shelley's anger, Mr Sixpence gave excuses that he had panicked after Shelley had threatened to take the farm from him but he promised to give Funny back his money and be the legal owner of the farm again.

After Shelley had given birth to a baby boy, Mr Sixpence waited only eight weeks before he made her pregnant again. Shelley named her first born son, Sixpence junior.

By the time Mr Sixpence turned ninety, his cash totalled five hundred and thirty nine billion pounds and Shelley could hardly wait to grab a hold of all that money. The only way she could obviously own the money was by getting rid of the owner who happened to be none other than the coin, Mr Sixpence. Mr Sixpence was a coin which never bought anything and his money was also money which never bought anything but Shelley was planning to start making sure that all that money would circulate.

Mr Sixpence kept his friends close but his enemies closest and that way it would then be easy for him to monitor their every move. One thing she should have always remembered was Sixpence the coin like all other real coins, had no blood running through his veins. Mr Sixpence cared for nobody except his money.

Mr Sixpence's other wives got fed up and annoyed with the way Shelley was being treated by their husband.

"Why should we be treated like second class citizens and Shelley get all his love, his time and his keys to the safe? It's not fair. We are also his legal wives never mind these toddlers that he his impregnating. You girls we should put a stop to this!" said Ju.

The unloved wives continued with their complaints and bit by bit began making life uneasy for Shelley. They stopped taking orders from Shelley and stopped talking to her completely. Little did they know that their true enemy was the coin itself. Shelley had also recently rediscovered that her husband had never taken the farm from his son, Funny. No legal work had been done concern the farm and that made Shelley very wrathful.

How could she have been so stupid as to believe that Mr Sixpence would repatriate funds? Once taken, any money that Mr Sixpence laid his hands on would never leave his safe.

As the Sixpence wives continued with their torturing games, Shelley also decided to take revenge by making sure the entire family go back to their one meal a day.

When asked by the wives Shelley replied, "I invented the three meals a day and now you convince your husband, the coin that you want three meals a day. Wish you lots of luck. You have been making my life a misery. Did you ever consider that I might also be a victim like the rest of you? I am trying to deal with caring for a blind mother, my baby, Sixpence junior who is still on the bottle and a pregnancy and how dare you attack me like this? How can an entire tribe help each other fight a helpless pregnant woman? When Sixpence dies, I will repossess this farm and if I were you, I would start looking for alternate accommodation" Shelley said and she left them mouthing and went to take a nap.

This kind of behaviour among his wives and children was affecting Mr Sixpence in a very negative way. He soon took ill and was admitted to hospital. The doctors at the hospital said he had a weak heart and was also suffering from fatigue which meant that his body was just tired and he needed rest.

"What do you expect, one man sharing the bed with a bunch of women and having to think for his numerous kids who seemed to use their intestines for reasoning All their problems had to be solved by their father. I hope he dies today" said Shelley.

"You are only saying that because your son is still a baby. Mr Sixpence never allows us to have a say in anything so it's not our children's fault if they don't use their brains at all. You leave us alone. We were a united family before you came and now you have changed our husband and he sees us as useless things….." said Ju as she wiped the tears of her cheeks and went on to say, "why did you come to this farm on the first place?"

"Do you know what Ju, it's you who should be dying and not him. Apparently this farm happens to belong to me. It so happens that my grandparents owned this farm and in fact it should be me asking you that very same question you just asked and if you say one more word, I will make sure you don't sleep there tonight, agreed?" replied Shelley.

CHAPTER TWENTY ONE

When Mr Sixpence thought he was about to go, he called his sons in private and asked them to change the lock to his safe. This was done behind Shelley's back and she still kept the safe keys which were now as useless as a suicidal person's pretty face which soon would be lying lifeless after crossing the thin line between life and death. Furthermore, according to nature or the Holy Bible, the pretty nose would sink on the fourth day after her death.

To cover up for his latest sins, Mr Sixpence continued to show more affection to Shelley. No one ever found out why in his last moments on planet earth, the coin was making sure his sons have his money after his death. It was only after his death that they realised that the truth of the matter was that he did not wish his sons to kill him if they discovered that even they themselves were not beneficiaries of his money. He was always scared of people screaming at him or hitting him, but preferred it the other way round and that was him attacking others instead.

The other Sixpence wives headed by Ju thought it best to kill Shelley because if she stayed alive, the farm would be hers. They plotted against her and called her to the storehouse on the pretext of needing cooking oil.

As soon as Shelley opened the door to the storehouse, two of the Sixpence wives grabbed her by the throat while the other wives beat her very hard. The ugliest wife whom Sixpence never bothered to talk to her day time but only share the bed with her in a dark room took a burning block of wood and hit her on one of her eyes. She must have meant to take out all her frustrations of being ill treated by Mr Sixpence.

"I don't deny the fact that I am ugly but I don't want it when someone like the coin makes it a point to remind me about my ugliness by not ignoring me Mr Sixpence will not and never has spoken to me in broad daylight. Do you know what that makes me feel? I took the liberty of asking him why he married me and he explained that at the pub we met, he was so drunk and not in his right mind and only realised it after I came here to break the news to him about my pregnancy. That's why I have removed your one eye because from now on your dearest won't want you near him!" everyone kept quiet after that except Shelley who was groaning in pain from all the beatings she had taken from her rivalries.

"Oh by the way, it's now like mother like daughter. How could you have sight when your mother is blind? All children should look like their parents" said another Sixpence crazy wife and they all burst out laughing.

Shelley was hospitalised for three months and returned back to her farm house looking a bit deformed.

-72-

Even though everybody disliked her, Shelley vowed she would never leave her grandmother's farm. By right, the farm belonged to her mother and to her because she was the legal guardian of her mother.

"Listen you master of cruelty, if you carry on loving Shelley more than us, we will definitely not hesitate to remove her one eye and she will be as blind as her mother!" threatened the angry wives as they spoke to their husband' Mr Sixpence.

"Mr Sixpence, our husband, you brought this upon yourself because like Shelley, we are your wives and to make matters worse, we have put up with you longer than her and most of your riches were earned by us. It's not only the fear of you loving Shelley but we know that you are facing death by age or by your illness and we are scared. Tell us where do you think we will go after you die?" asked Ju.

For the sake of peace, Shelley thought it wise to share duties with Mr Sixpence's other wives.

CHAPTER TWENTY TWO

One fine day as Shelley was coming from attending to her needy mother, she made plans to go and check on toilet rolls in the storehouse.

On her way to the storehouse, she accidentally dropped the supposedly safe keys.

When the other wives noticed that Shelley had keys, they got very annoyed but this time they decided not to hit Shelley but take it out on Mr Sixpence himself. They just had taken more than enough from this old man.

"We actually made it so clear to him that we had to be treated the same but he never seemed to understand our feelings. Anyway, how can a one-eyed wife see clearly where she is going? I have an idea, why don't we all team up and visit the hospital where we will all give the coin a lesson for life. It seems to me that only death will stop all this nonsense going on in our lives. As for me I have had enough and I can't take anymore. I don't even have feelings for him because the last time he shared my bed with me was the time when I was breastfeeding my Timothy and now Timothy is a grown man with his own wife and two children. To me, Mr Sixpence died twenty years ago. Come on let's go girls!" said Timothy's mum.

They were lucky enough to find the coin in the hospital grounds busking in the sun. Ju was the first one to slap him on his cheek and the rest of the wives joined in by hitting him so hard that after a few minutes, the coin lay motionless in the hospital garden. They checked his pulse and realised that he was still breathing.

"The witch is like a cat which has nine lives. You mean to tell me that after all that beating he is still alive. I think Shelley's idea was the best – use rat poison and not just one spoon but empty the entire contents" said Ju, feeling very defeated.

The hospital staff came after one of the patients found Mr Sixpence's body lying down with no one around as his crazy wives had escaped in fear of the police. Mr Sixpence was rushed to the theatre for the surgical operation on his entire body.

Mr Sixpence survived the surgical operation and was taken to Intensive Care Unit. Although he had regained consciousness, Mr Sixpence was given a few days to live by his doctor.

During his last moments, Mr Sixpence sent for his solicitor and told him that he wanted to make a will. Mr Sixpence also told his solicitor that he wanted his will to be read to his family while his body was still in the mortuary before his burial.

Mr Sixpence's will read;

THEME: NOBODY TOUCHES MY MONEY

FIRST OF ALL TO MY SONS WHO ARE IN THE CREMATORIUM BUSINESS, PLEASE FIND CARPENTERS WHO WILL BE ABLE TO MANUFACTURE A COFFIN BIG ENOUGH AND WIDE ENOUGH TO ACCOMMODATE MY DEAD BODY INCLUDING ALL THE MONEY IN MY UNDERGROUND SAFE. DON'T FORGET TO PUT ALL THE GOLD AND JEWELLERY HIDDEN BENEATH THE BOX CONTAINING ALL MY MONEY.

AFTER THE COFFIN IS MADE AND ALL MY JEWELERY LAID AT THE BOTTOM OF THE COFFIN, PUT ALL MY MONEY ON TOP OF THE JEWELLERY THEN MY BODY LAST. LASTLY, SEAL MY COFFIN AND THEN ASK MY CHILDREN WHO DIG PEOPLE'S GRAVES TO DIG A GRAVE WIDE ENOUGH AND DEEP ENOUGH TO PUT MY COFFIN.

AFTER BURYING ME, MAKE SURE YOU PUT TAR ON TOP OF MY GRAVE THAT VERY SAME DAY OF MY BURIAL.

THE FARM AND ALL ITS CONTENTS WERE SOLD TO MY SON, FUNNY AND HIS NAME IS ALREADY ON THE TITLE DEEDS.

AS FOR MY FAVOURITE WIFE SHELLEY, I JUST HAVE THIS TO SAY 'HAD YOU NOT THREATENED TO KILL ME, I WOULD HAVE LEFT SOME MONEY FOR YOU. YOUR BEST OPTION SHELLEY, WOULD BE TO MARRY FUNNY, BUT ONLY MARRY HIM IF HIS FIRST WIFE IS AGREEABLE TO THAT KIND OF LIVING',

AFTER I AM GONE, MY ADVICE TO YOU MY FAMILY IS: WORK HARD FOR YOUR OWN MONEY LIKE I DID WHILE I WAS ALIVE.

I WAS A SHINING EXAMPLE TO YOU MY WIVES AND PLEASE BE GOOD EXAMPLES TO YOUR OFFSPRING

THE DAY I AM BURIED IS THE DAY YOU ALL VACATE THE FARM BECAUSE FUNNY'S WIFE DOES NOT LIKE TOO MANY PEOPLE AROUND YOU.

THUS WITTEN AND SIGNED BY ME THE COIN:

FIRST NAME : COIN
SURNAME: SIXPENCE
SIGNED; C SIXPENCE

THIS 30TH DAY OF DECEMBER

An hour later, after writing and signing his will, Mr Coin Sixpence gave up the ghost and the will was read to his family as per his request.

The Sixpences wives cursed and cried and came to a point where they wanted to hit his dead body.

"How and where will we go if he is going to be buried with his every dime and nickel?" each family member asked the other.

"You are worrying about sleeping arrangements only, what about me? I spent twenty five years begging for money from strangers whilst pretending to be a blind person. The coin told me that he was saving my money and I would get it if anything happened to me. I cold have been arrested for fraud. Listen, I want my money and if not I will call the cops!" said one of Mr Sixpence's widows.

"No wonder he used you because you are very stupid. What are you going to tell the cops? 1. The money is not in your name and I think you will be arrested instead for claiming money that does not belong to you. 2. You got that money using deceitful ideas. The people who gave you that money will have you and the law will also have you for confirming with your own mouth that you pretended to be blind and the last thing we are all dreading to hear is that it was Mr Sixpence's idea which enabled you to earn all that money. Shut up and come up with some sensible ideas because we only have a few hours before that money goes sixty feet deep!" said Ju.

“How about us, his own daughters, we caught diseases selling our bodies and him there keeping all the money!” said one of his daughters and they hugged each other and cried until their eyes were swollen.

“Again, it was his idea for you to sell your bodies. You girls should have married all those rich men you were entertaining” said Ju.

“Whose side are you on anyway? That beast you are praising is dead and you need his signature to get any money you may need to sustain you for the rest of your life.

Ju, who seemed to be under shock opened her mouth again and said, “I am only telling you facts. I, myself was a rough sleeper and this man improved my life as bad as you all want him to be. The best idea would be to kill the solicitor and act as if no will was written.”

“I think the coin is getting more popular after his death. Do you know what he asked the solicitor to do? Copies of his will were sent to Funny and the headquaters of the mafia gang where he was a member. My best advice is we all die because as dead people, we do not need money for anything except worry about rotting in hell. Ju, where is that preacher of yours. I need to go and confess my sins and then ask God to kill me because I will be assured a place in Heaven” said the ugly wife.

“Ho, ho ho ho ho, wait a minute, I myself, don’t mind burning his coffin and removing the money before I do so. That dead man who so happens to be my biological father is evil. That man does not deserve a decent burial. Do you want to know why? Ask me and I will tell you. I spent lots of my nights doing the dirty jobs of emptying coffins after the relatives of the dead had laid to rest their departed loved ones. My half brothers and I here sold all those coffins to our friends and we have to live with that guilt. Honestly speaking, that money belongs to us and not to him. He never worked but we his family worked to raise all that money which will be six feet under very soon” said one of his sons.

“Like I said, the police will arrest you at the mention of stealing coffins and worse still all your neighbours will either kill you or take revenge which will affect your entire future. The best thing is to bury him according to his will and I regret to say this but we should have allowed Shelley to poison him that time she wanted to. We were stupid enough to warn him. Wherever I go, if I ever manage to go anywhere at all, I will live with this guilt of stopping Shelley kill him. Shelley is just a moody person but very kind. She would never see us on the streets” said Ju.

“One more word of discouragement from you and I will silence you Ju. I mean it!” said the ugly widow.

"Never mind Ju's comments and let's go back to reality. It's hard enough to think of our long term future but what about the immediate problem? Can anyone educate me as to what we are going to eat today and tomorrow with people gathering in our farm to mourn the coin?" asked one of Mr Sixpence's widows.

Anyway, soon after burying their father, according to his will, the Sixpence widows and children spit on his grave and cursed it and then disappeared from the farm.
Nobody ever knew where they went and no one seemed to bother. Some said it was good riddance to bad rubbish as the Sixpence family had contributed nothing to society except scrounge or steal from everybody else. Legend has it that ninety nine percent had been cremated by the crematorium boys.

On the other hand, one-eyed Shelley and her mother stayed on the farm waiting for Funny Sixpence and his wife to arrive.

The graveyard crew had put some special engravings on the grave of their biological father.

It had this on it: **GM10**

GOD MADE MEN

MEN MADE MONEY

MONEY MADE

MANY MEN MAD

THE SIXPENCE COIN LOVED MONEY MORE THAN US

According to his family and neighbours that was the end of terror as Mr Sixpence had terrorised everybody even the ones who loved him never mind the ones he had been authorised by the Creator, to put on planet earth. His own children!

LAST CHAPTER

As per the contents of the will made by the late Mr Sixpence, Funny and his wife arrived at the farm for the purposes of owning it.

Shelley played it cool but had other crazy ideas to get rid of Funny.

A copy of Mr Sixpence's will had been given to Shelley by Mr Sixpence's solicitor. Shelley had taken the liberty of altering it to read: *FUNNY WILL ONLY OWN THE FARM IF HE MARRIES SHELLEY.*

Because he was as greedy as his late father, Funny agreed to marry Shelley as polygamy was very legal in their country. Funny wanted to have children with Shelley since his first wife was barren but Shelley had secretly visited her doctor and had persuaded him to have her tubes tied. Shelley did not want to promote Mr Sixpence's blood running through any living beings.

Luckily enough, Shelley had not gotten rid of the poison she had meant to use on her late husband. When Shelley thought her time was up, she made plans to kill Funny on his birthday. A birthday party was arranged and the party began. Actually Shelley was celebrating the death of her enemy and the beginning of her freedom.

"I have never seen you so happy. What's up? I know the reason you are so overjoyed – it's not only about my birthday but you are pregnant aren't you?" said Funny as he hugged his wife and carried on drinking his whisky which his wife had bought for him.

While all the guests were busy drinking and dancing, Shelley went to her kitchen and took out the small bottle containing rat poison. She opened it and quickly empted it into the big pot of soup on her cooker.

A few minutes later everyone at the party was complaining of tummy aches. Ambulances were called and they were all rushed to hospital. Unfortunately there were no survivors.

The cops decided to treat the deaths of Funny and the guests who died attending his birthday as a homicide case. Shelley got a phone call from the police and they told her that they were coming to her farm to carry investigations.

On realising the charges she faced if the police proved she had killed thirty three people, Shelley took her late husband's shotgun and first shot her mum and children dead and then put a bullet through her head and that became the end of the Sixpences.

It had been Mr Sixpence's dream that no living human being touch or use anything belonging to him and true to his will and his desires, **nobody ever owned that farm after Mr Coin Sixpence died, not even his friends. Witches worldwide believe his money is still buried in his big coffin with him. WHO DARE OPEN HIS COFFIN AND SUFFER BAD LUCK LIKE HIS OWN FAMILY WHO DIED DURING THE PROCESS OF TRYING TO TAKE WHAT BELONGED TO THE SIXPENCE COIN?**

THE VERY END

www.ingramcontent.com/pod-product-compliance
Ingram Content Group UK Ltd.
Pitfield, Milton Keynes, MK11 3LW, UK
UKHW021528300726
14060UKWH00011B/27

9 781471 698804